ANIMAL INVESTIGATORS:

MISSION 1

RED EYE

The gulls parted. And for a moment, he saw a tiny staggering figure, flapping its arms wildly about. Then the screeching gull pack, like a great evil white cloud, closed again over its head.

"They're driving him out onto the mudflats!" said Danny. "He'll get stuck. He'll drown!"

The great gull pack was breaking up, wheeling away. Their work was done. And now there was just a tiny figure, alone in the middle of the bay. It struggled. But it seemed to be stuck in the mud. And the tide was speeding in like a bullet train.

"We have to help him," said Ellis.

SUSAN GATES worked as a teacher in Africa and then in England before becoming a full-time writer. She has since had over one hundred books published and, among other prizes, has won the Sheffield Book Award twice and been commended for the Carnegie Medal.

Susan is married with a daughter and two sons, and lives in County Durham.

ANIMAL INVESTIGATORS: MISSION 1

RED EYE

SUSAN GATES

USBORNE

To Laura, Alex
and Chris

First published in the UK in 2007 by Usborne Publishing Ltd.,
Usborne House, 83-85 Saffron Hill, London EC1N 8RT, England.
www.usborne.com

Copyright © Susan Gates, 2007

The right of Susan Gates to be identified as the author of this work
has been asserted by her in accordance with the Copyright, Designs
and Patents Act, 1988.

The name Usborne and the devices ♀ ⊕ are Trade Marks of
Usborne Publishing Ltd.

This is a work of fiction. The characters, incidents, and dialogues are
products of the author's imagination and are not to be construed as real.
Any resemblance to actual events or persons, living or dead, is entirely
coincidental.

A CIP catalogue record for this book is available from the British Library.

JFMA JJASOND/07   ISBN 9780746085752   Printed in Great Britain.

The boy thought, *I've made it!*

He could hardly believe it. He touched the wounds on his neck and winced. He'd been seen by one of their sentries. They had eyes everywhere; watched everything you did. The sentry had attacked him savagely, slashed his neck, tried to drive him back to the town. But then the fog had come rolling in and saved him.

The boy was running now, through thick, white fog. He couldn't see more than a metre ahead. He could hear waves crashing on either side of him, smell rotting seaweed. One wrong step and he'd be swept away. But he was okay – so long as he stayed on this narrow strip of land that curved out into the ocean like a crooked finger. That had his forgotten little town, Mackenzie Point, right on its very tip.

But even while he was thinking, *I've escaped!* he was still afraid. These days, everyone in Mackenzie Point lived in fear, terrified of breaking the rules, of being punished, or even *disappeared,* like the Mayor.

It was six kilometres to the mainland. Then he caught a bus, to Clayborough, the nearest big town. By the time the boy reached it, the fog had cleared. He looked round, amazed. He felt unreal. Everything here seemed so *normal*. He'd forgotten what that was like.

People in Clayborough were driving cars, shopping; kids were skateboarding. No one was shuffling around, scared even to lift their heads.

Suddenly the boy thought, *What if* they've *followed me?* Had the sentry seen which direction he'd taken, before the fog closed in? If he had, he'd have reported back to headquarters.

Shivering, the boy dared to lift his eyes, look into the sky. It was clear blue and empty. He couldn't see them on the rooftops either. If *they* were hunting him down, that's where they'd be. But he wasn't reassured. Anyone who broke the rules suffered; he'd seen it with his own eyes. And when *they* took revenge, it was ruthless.

He scurried on, his heart racing.

He stood on the railway platform, waiting for the 8 a.m. fast train to the city. People gave him sneaky glances. Then he realized that, apart from his bleeding neck, he still had his crash helmet on.

He took it off, pulled up his collar to hide his injuries. Tried to look like normal. Like any kid on a holiday trip to the city, maybe to do some shopping, go to the cinema. But he couldn't stop his hands shaking. His guts felt like a knot of worms. His eyes were flickering all over the place. He felt he was only just holding it together. He was scared for himself. But scared, as well, for his friends back in Mackenzie Point. They could be punished, because he'd escaped. And if they tried to hide, someone would inform on them. That's what it was like in his town now. You couldn't trust anyone. Not even your own relatives.

He wanted to blurt out to these people: "I'm from Mackenzie Point. Do you know what's happening to us out there?"

How could they seem so happy, so unconcerned? Going about their daily business, when, in his town, they were living a nightmare?

But he didn't breathe a word. There was only one person he was going to tell. One person who'd helped him before in a life or death situation. Who'd given him wise advice. He was going to the city now, to find him.

The train appeared round a curve in the track, slid into Clayborough station.

He'll help us, thought the boy, as he climbed aboard with the other passengers. *Professor Talltrees will know what to do*.

CHAPTER TWO

Ellis Straker and Meriel were out in the garden, behind the city's Natural History Museum. Mealworms wriggled on Meriel's outstretched palm. She was feeding them to a robin.

"So what's it thinking?" asked Ellis.

Meriel said, "It's thinking, *I'm boss of this garden.* It's thinking, *These stupid humans are late with my breakfast.*"

"Come on," said Ellis. "You never did the trance thing."

Like Ellis, Meriel was thirteen years old. She was small, quick, dark-haired. She looked like any ordinary girl. Except there was something odd about her. You could see it in her eyes – the way they flashed sometimes, were wild and not quite human. Meriel could think herself inside the minds of animals. But she wasn't doing it this morning.

"You were just guessing," Ellis accused her.

"So?" Meriel shrugged, impatiently. "What's to know about what a robin's thinking? Robins are dumb. All birds are dumb." She darted off to another part of the garden.

Ellis sighed. He knew the signs. Meriel was getting restless again. She got like that after being cooped up in the city for too long. She needed space, to roam wild and free. If she didn't get it, she would just take off by herself.

Better warn the Prof, thought Ellis.

Except Prof. Talltrees didn't seem too concerned when Meriel did one of her disappearing acts. Other guardians would panic, report a missing person. But the Prof just said, "She'll be back."

Suddenly, Ellis dropped to one knee. In an instant he'd forgotten about Meriel. He was totally focused on the footprints he'd found in the soggy lawn. He touched the mud, rubbed it through his fingers. They were fresh footprints, made minutes ago. He knew one of the sets of prints well enough. Size eleven trainers, with the right foot dragging because the wearer had a limp.

"Hey," he told Meriel. "The Prof's just been out here."

Usually their guardian didn't appear until lunchtime. He'd be down in the dusty corridors under the Natural History Museum, surrounded by bones, doing research into extinct animals.

Ellis studied the other prints. He was quieter than Meriel, less volatile, more watchful. His grey eyes were steady. And they didn't miss a thing. They saw all the tiny details other people miss – the claw scratch on the bark, the thread of clothing on a bush. Ellis was a tracker. He'd been trained by a master tracker in Africa to read the signs left by animals and people. That was before his parents got killed by poachers two years ago and he came to live with Prof. Talltrees.

Ellis shook his head to drive out thoughts of his parents.

"The Prof's got someone with him," he told Meriel. "A stranger."

She came over, stared at the footprints. "And?" she said. She might be able to think herself into the minds of animals. But the footprints were just marks in the mud to her.

"It's a boy," said Ellis. "Size six shoes, maybe our age. Maybe a bit younger."

He could have told Meriel the stranger's weight, his height. Except she'd already darted off. He could tell something else about the stranger too. He'd been pacing about, jittery, tensed up.

Like there's something big on his mind. Like he's scared or something, thought Ellis.

Then he frowned. His eagle-sharp eyes had seen a single red drop.

"There's blood here," he murmured. "Somebody's injured."

His ears picked up the faint crunch of gravel. Instantly his senses were on full alert. He melted into the trees and stayed there, perfectly still, hardly breathing.

"Ellis? Meriel? Are you out here?" called Professor Talltrees.

Ellis slid out of the trees. The Prof didn't flinch. He was used to Ellis sneaking up on people, appearing out of nowhere. But the boy with him almost jumped out of his skin.

Knew he was jittery, thought Ellis.

Meriel came running up. They both stared at the boy. An old motorbike crash helmet dangled from one hand. There were two slash wounds on his neck. One crusty with dried blood. One bleeding, because he'd picked at it.

Made maybe five, six hours ago, guessed Ellis, looking at them with a tracker's eye.

And the boy himself seemed like his nerves were shattered. He was permanently cringing. Every so often, he glanced up into the sky. Then glanced away as if looking up wasn't allowed.

Prof. Talltrees, tall, gangling, grey-haired, stood beside him. He wore a black eyepatch over his left eye. Scars, from an old wound, ran from beneath it, right down to his chin.

"This is Danny Dillon," he said. "I think you'll be interested in what he's got to tell you."

Then he limped off, back to his bones, in the basement of the Natural History Museum.

Danny gazed after him, appalled. He'd expected the Prof to help. He'd come all this way, at dreadful risk, especially to see him. Now he felt like he'd been abandoned.

He stared at the boy and girl the Prof had left him with.

They're just two kids like me, thought Danny in despair. *How can they be any help?*

Chapter Three

It was a year ago when Danny and the Prof first made contact. Danny had been walking down the street in Mackenzie Point.

There was a seagull chick. Right there, in the middle of the pavement. He'd almost stepped on it. It was just a little grey ball of fluff. Danny had crouched down.

"Hey," he'd said. "What are you doing here?"

It seemed to have fallen out of the sky. They were used to seagulls in Mackenzie Point, screeching and swooping overhead. But they didn't live in the town; they nested on an old iron fort out at sea, hundreds of them. Was this one from there? It must have been snatched from its nest, then dropped. Another gull could have done it. Danny knew gulls were cannibals – that they ate their own kind.

Danny had picked it up.

"Ow!"

It was tiny but a real fighter. It had struggled, tried to stab him with its beak. It had already been leg ringed, with a black band. That meant it probably came not from the fort, but from the Wild Bird Reserve down the coast.

He'd taken it home and called it Jet. But he'd had no idea how to keep it alive. It wouldn't feed. On the second day, it couldn't even lift its head. And it had been clear to Danny that Jet was dying.

So he'd e-mailed Prof. Talltrees. It was out of sheer desperation. He'd never even heard of the Prof before. But he'd happened to catch the end of an old programme of his on local telly, about caring for wild birds.

"He's the guy I want," Danny had told Mum, all excited. "He works at that big museum place in the city – the programme said so. I'm going to e-mail him right now about Jet!"

"Well, don't get your hopes up," said Danny's mum. "He used to be on telly a lot – he was a world-famous wildlife expert. But then he had some kind of bad accident. After that he just dropped out of sight. I haven't heard about him for years. You sure he's still alive?"

But to her surprise the Prof was still very much alive. Danny had got an e-mail back from him inside an hour, like the Prof recognized it was an emergency. He told Danny how to care for Jet, how to feed him, first from an eye dropper, then with cat food. And, because of the Prof, Jet survived. He'd grown into a handsome bird, a Great Black-backed Gull. He and Danny had become inseparable. People in Mackenzie Point got used to Danny and his tame gull. When you saw Danny Dillon, Jet was always fluttering somewhere behind.

Danny went to a high school on the mainland. Granddad took him across every day by boat. And every day, when they came chugging back, Jet would be waiting for him on the dock.

Jet thought he was human. Danny's mum had said, "I swear that gull understands every word I say."

But, a few weeks later, there'd been an awful scene. Jet had done his usual trick, swooping over the garden, sicking up an oily, foul-smelling mess of food. But this time, it had gone on Mum's clean washing.

She'd gone berserk! "I hate that bird," she'd screamed.

"He's just regurgitating," Danny had said. "All gulls do that."

But Mum was having a bad day. Danny knew the signs. Soon, she'd get itchy feet – she'd go off travelling somewhere, leave him with Granddad like she always did.

"Did you hear me?" she'd screeched, her voice loud enough to shatter glass. "It's noisy. It stinks. Get rid of it!"

"Besides," she'd said later when she'd calmed down. "It should go back to the wild."

So Danny had stopped feeding Jet. The gull kept coming back to the garden. It had wrenched Danny's heart to see him, just sitting there, on top of the garage, waiting. But he knew Mum was right. Jet had to look after himself.

"Go away!" Danny had shouted. He'd run outside, picked up some gravel, chucked it in Jet's direction. Jet had sat there for a second, as if he couldn't quite believe what Danny was doing.

"Go away!" Danny had shouted, tears choking his voice. "And don't come back!"

Finally, Jet had flapped his great wings and swooped away, over the rooftops.

And he never came back. As if he'd realized that he wasn't human after all, that he belonged with the other gulls.

Danny wondered how Jet felt about people now. Danny imagined him hating them, feeling cast-out, betrayed.

Wonder how he feels about me? Danny thought. But he decided, *Me and Jet will always be friends. No matter what.* He really wanted to believe that.

He knew he'd done the right thing. It wasn't much consolation though. He missed Jet terribly.

But, standing here, with Ellis and Meriel, in the garden of the city's Natural History Museum, Danny wasn't going to waste time on Jet's story. Besides,

Jet wasn't the one causing the problem. It was all the others.

"Gulls have moved into our town, loads of them," Danny told Ellis and Meriel. "It's 'cos the iron fort where they lived got demolished. And the garbage boats got stopped."

That had been the gulls' main food source – the rotting rubbish taken by barges to be dumped at sea.

"So?" interrupted Meriel, rudely. She was already starting to wander off again.

"Wait," Ellis stopped her. "We should at least *listen* to him, like the Prof said. Let's take him inside. He looks done in."

Meriel shrugged. She wasn't the sympathetic type, at least not where people were concerned. But, like Ellis, she had respect for Prof. Talltrees. Apart from Ellis, he was the only person whose opinions she cared much about. So she sighed and said, "Okay. I suppose we've got to."

Danny licked his dry lips, tried not to scratch his neck. He looked nervously from one of them to the other. He felt like a total outsider. There were looks passing between them he couldn't interpret; some kind of bond he didn't understand. Especially, he didn't like that girl. She seemed haughty, unfriendly. But he trailed after them into the huge, rambling, grey stone museum. He didn't know what else to do.

"Want something to eat?" asked Ellis, when they were sitting in the kitchen of Prof. Talltrees's basement apartment.

Danny shook his head. He was starving hungry but food didn't matter. All that mattered was making them take him seriously. Making them see that the people in his tiny community of Mackenzie Point desperately needed help.

"So where is this place Mackenzie Point? I've never heard of it," said Meriel, squirming in her seat, as if at any moment she might leap up and dash away. "What's it like?"

That didn't seem important to Danny. But he told her anyway – there was something about her intense and challenging stare that really unnerved him. Like she was sizing him up as prey.

"Er," said Danny, fumbling for the words. He thought about how others might see his home town. "Er, it's way out on a headland, like at the end of the world. It's a little seaside place – a bit of a dump, really."

He thought of the spooky Wonderland, closed and half-derelict, where gulls roosted in rows on the roller coaster and helter-skelter. Of the Town Hall, that they'd made their HQ. Of the Mayor, just disappearing, vanishing off the face of the earth...

But that would be rushing too fast with his story.

So he just said, "No one goes to Mackenzie Point now. You can't take cars over any more, it's not safe. And most people that lived there have moved away. That's 'cos the whole place is falling into the sea. Some houses have already slid in."

And soon, the sea would swallow up the road, their only link with the mainland, and they'd be cut off altogether.

"Sounds lovely," yawned Meriel, fiddling with a salt pot.

Danny thought, *This is a waste of time*. But Prof. Talltrees had told him to tell his story to these two weirdos. And Danny was in awe of the Prof. Firstly, because his wisdom about gulls had saved Jet's life. But also because of his appearance. Danny hadn't expected those awful scars and eyepatch. The Prof hadn't had those on the telly programme. They must be from the accident Mum had talked about.

Danny's mind started drifting. He wondered where Jet was right now. He thought he'd spotted him once or twice with the other gulls. But he couldn't be sure.

"Danny?" said Ellis, gently. "Hey, Danny." He could see the boy was lost in his own private nightmare. You didn't need to be a top tracker to tell that he'd been deeply traumatized by something.

Meriel said, "I've got things to do." She sprang out of her seat.

Ellis shot an angry glance at her. He told Danny. "*I'm* listening, anyway."

"Huh," said Meriel, scornfully. "Gulls."

Then a cool, quiet voice from the doorway said, "The Great Black-backed Gull has got a wingspan of nearly two metres."

Prof. Talltrees came limping in. Something had made him come back and listen in to the conversation.

"He can swallow rats whole," continued the Prof, "take cats from gardens, attack, even kill people with his claws and beak. When he feeds, he's voracious. He can snatch a puffin out of the sky, turn it inside out with a few shakes of his beak and gobble up its guts."

"Inside out?" said Meriel, impressed.

She sat back down on her chair. It seemed she was listening now. As if she thought a bird like that deserved some respect.

"That's what he is!" Danny burst out. "Red Eye! He's a Great Black-backed Gull!"

Just like Jet. Only Red Eye was bigger than Jet. He was the biggest gull Danny had ever seen.

"Who's Red Eye?" asked Ellis.

"He's the Boss. They all do what he says."

"Look," said Ellis, as Prof. Talltrees leaned against the wall, listening. "Maybe you'd better start from the beginning."

Danny swivelled round, shot a beseeching look at Prof. Talltrees as if to say, *Do I have to talk to these two kids. It's you I came to see.*

Prof. Talltrees said, "I don't go out into the field any more. My work here on extinct animals takes up all my time. I send Ellis and Meriel instead. They're my representatives. They act on my behalf. And they have my complete trust."

"Okay," said Danny, doubtfully. He still didn't see how two kids could help. Although maybe, just maybe, there was something about them – Ellis

Straker's steady gaze and quiet watchfulness. And that Meriel. She gave him the creeps – like she wasn't quite human. But she had such a proud and insolent stare, as if nothing could get the better of *her*.

So he turned back to face them, tried to pull himself together. He needed to get this story right. He had to convince them that terrible things were happening in Mackenzie Point. That their little community was being torn apart.

"Well, at first the gulls were just a nuisance," Danny told them. "They screamed all day long. Nicked people's ice-cream cones, stuff like that."

"Nicked your ice-cream cone?" said Meriel. "Gosh, they sound really dangerous."

Prof. Talltrees flashed her a look, that said, *Come on, give him a chance.*

But Danny didn't seem to have heard her. He seemed hypnotized by his story. "They pulled things out of rubbish bins, chucked them about. Yellow bins," he told them. "They attacked yellow bins. Yellow bins drove them crazy..."

"Yellow bins?" Meriel mouthed to Ellis, raising her eyebrows. They both grinned.

"Yeah and they crapped on people's heads." Danny was rushing on. "That's Zapper. He never misses."

"You've got names for them?" asked Ellis, surprised.

"Oh, yeah," said Danny. "Some of them, anyway. There's Zapper, and Snapper and Hook Beak and Silver Back." He threw an apologetic glance at the Prof's eyepatch. "And there's Pirate, 'cos he's got a brown ring round his eye. They're all Red Eye's bodyguard..."

"Bodyguard?" said Meriel, wrinkling her nose in disbelief.

"Anyway," Danny went on in a rush of words, "I'm talking about when they first came. Right? They started to snatch food, like crisps, from kids' hands, things like that. Just swoop down and snatch them. Then they started clawing people's heads – I mean really vicious. People had blood running down their faces! So the Mayor got mad. It was war, like, 'Let's wipe 'em all out!' He even shot at Red Eye with his air rifle! But the gulls fought back. This old guy, they attacked him, when he was raking their nests off his roof. He fell off his ladder. Then the Mayor disappeared..."

"Disappeared?" said Ellis. "You think the gulls had something to do with it?"

"Course they did!" said Danny.

"Come on!" said Ellis in amazement. "You expect us to believe that?"

"They disappeared Mrs. Wilson's cat, Bilbo!" protested Danny. "They did it to punish her!"

Mrs. Wilson fed Bilbo some tinned cat food. Cat food she should have given to the gulls. The gulls found out – Red Eye had spies all over the place. And the next day, they came for Bilbo. He just vanished, into thin air.

But Danny didn't tell the whole story. What was the use? Ellis and Meriel still wouldn't understand. No one could who hadn't lived in Mackenzie Point for the last few weeks. Danny had been there. But even he couldn't believe how quickly it had happened.

"Look," Danny begged, desperately, "just please come and help us, please. Please..."

Danny couldn't speak. They could see he was close to tears. Meriel looked away, embarrassed. Ellis reached out. "Want a drink?" Danny accepted the glass of water gratefully, gulped it down.

"This Red Eye?" Ellis started to ask.

Danny burst out, before he could finish the question, "He's really big, I mean, bigger than the other Great Black-backeds. And he hasn't got a black back – he's white all over with red eyes and he's clever, he plans things."

"Plans?" Meriel leaned forward on her chair. "Come on, you're kidding me."

"No, honest!" said Danny, frantic to make them believe.

Ellis was privately thinking, *This kid is crazy*. But he asked another question. "This place you live in, it's tiny, cut-off, right? But there's mobiles, e-mails. Why did nobody call for help?"

"There's no mobile reception," said Danny, "and no electricity since they dropped rocks in the wind turbines, smashed up the blades." But Danny knew it wasn't just that. "No one dares," he told them. "No one dares call for help. And no one can leave. Unless you're a Creeper. And even then, you've got to get permission."

"Creeper?" questioned Ellis.

"Permission?" said Meriel. "From a seagull?"

They're laughing at me, thought Danny.

"Look, I can't explain everything!" he burst out. "Creepers, they help the gulls. They've like, gone over to their side! They even wrecked our boats – except for a few. And only they're allowed to use those."

Ellis shot an incredulous look at Meriel. She shrugged. She could hardly believe all this either. But that bit about the intelligent gull – could it really be true? If it was, she'd like to meet it, get inside its mind.

Danny turned again to Prof. Talltrees. "Tell them to come!" he demanded. "Make them come! You've got to."

"Actually," said the Prof, with the faintest smile, "it's their choice."

Ellis glanced at Meriel. He saw her eyes sparkling. He knew those signs. She was excited.

"We'll think about it," he told Danny.

Danny went to the bathroom to clean up, put some antiseptic on his wounds. Prof. Talltrees, Ellis and Meriel discussed him.

"Think he's telling the truth?" said Ellis. "About this Red Eye?"

The Prof frowned. "I don't know. It's obviously some kind of mutant gull. It's an albino for a start, white all over with pink eyes. Albinos are always unpredictable. Their brains are wired differently from other animals."

"But super intelligent?" protested Ellis. "Danny's got to be kidding!"

The Prof shook his head. "Doesn't sound likely, does it? A really bright gull would be self aware, like people are."

"What do you mean?" asked Ellis.

"Well, when you look at your reflection in a mirror you know it's you, don't you?"

"Yeah, sure." Ellis shrugged.

"Well, birds don't. They don't have the brainpower. They just think it's another bird and attack it."

"Okay. So if this Red Eye recognizes its own reflection, we should be worried?"

"Oh yes," said Prof. Talltrees. "Because that would show you're dealing with a very smart bird. A bird that can think like you do."

Ellis laughed. "Yeah, well, let's get real. That's not going to happen, is it?"

"So do you want to go?" asked the Prof.

It wasn't the first mission the pair had been on.

His wards made a formidable team. Meriel, especially, had extraordinary powers. The Prof knew they could take care of themselves, better than most adults. Better than he could with his lame leg – he'd just slow them down. He knew, too, that before they became his wards, they were both used to freedom. Even if he'd wanted to, he couldn't keep them reined in. Meriel didn't obey rules. Not human rules, anyway.

But, all the same, he couldn't help worrying. There were lots of dangers out there. Ellis was more logical, level-headed. But Meriel could be reckless. She was more vulnerable than she thought. Sometimes, she took crazy risks.

And he had an uneasy feeling about this mission. "Look, I don't know if it's true about this Red Eye," he said. "Or if the gulls were involved in the Mayor's disappearance. But *something* strange is happening in that little town."

"Huh!" said Meriel. "Bet that Danny's making a big fuss about nothing. But it might be fun. And anyway, I was getting bored."

Ellis glanced at the Prof, raised his eyebrows. When Meriel got bored they'd all better watch out.

Something moved under her jacket.

Her pet weasel, Travis, poked out his silky red head. His glittering eyes scanned the room. He was part of the menagerie of creatures Meriel kept in her room, for company. He rippled over the table, quick and sinuous as a snake and out of the cat flap in the back door. He was going hunting. Weasels are ferocious hunters. They take on prey much bigger than themselves, even badgers and wolves if they're cornered. And they never, ever surrender. Meriel had a lot of time for weasels.

She rushed to the window and watched Travis. He leaped through the long grass, his body arching like a tiny red rainbow. She closed her eyes, concentrated. And suddenly, she was inside his mind, his body, feeling what he felt, smelling what he smelled, seeing through his eyes. Grass brushed her furry coat as she whisked by. A dew drop sparkled. Pebbles and twigs seemed giant-sized.

Then there was darkness, earth. Travis was down a rat's hole. A musty rat smell; he'd scented prey. Meriel saw bared yellow teeth, tasted blood, heard it squeal. In her trance, she shivered with excitement, feeling Travis's power and wildness...

Someone shook her, broke the spell. It was Ellis. "Meriel? Stop messing about."

In a second she'd lost the connection. She was back to herself, in her own body.

"There's no time for that," said Ellis. "Come on, we've got to pack some stuff. We're going to Mackenzie Point."

The three of them, Ellis, Meriel and Danny, left the city museum. They had a long journey ahead of them. First the train, then bus, then the walk out to Mackenzie Point. It would be dark before they got there.

"But we need the dark," said Danny. He was already worrying about how he was going to smuggle them in without the sentries seeing.

But, as they hurried through the streets to the train station, he didn't feel quite as frenzied and hopeless as before. At first, he'd had no faith in Meriel and Ellis. He thought he'd made a wasted journey. And he knew they had no idea yet what they were taking on. But when they'd agreed to come he'd felt weak with relief. Like the responsibility for saving Mackenzie Point had somehow shifted off his shoulders.

On the train, Danny slept the whole way, exhausted. He only woke up when Ellis shook him and said, "We're at Clayborough. Isn't this where we get off?"

With Meriel and Ellis beside him, he stumbled out into the town streets. He forgot to look up into the sky, checking for gulls.

He should have done.

Up on the station roof, there was a sudden flurry of huge feathery wings. It might have been an angel. Only it croaked, *"Ka, ka ka!"* in a harsh, most unangel-like voice. And, beside it, on the ledge, were what remained of its last meal – the skin of a pigeon, neatly turned inside out.

And when it took off, a black ring flashed on its scaly leg.

CHAPTER FOUR

Above the tiny seaside town of Mackenzie Point, the air was full of gulls: herring gulls mostly or black-headed gulls. They swirled in clouds, squabbled and fought. Their feathers drifted like snow down into the streets below.

Often, they swooped back to their main nesting site in Wonderland, carrying food. The old roller coaster was white with their droppings. Every ledge was crammed with untidy heaps of sticks. And in each heap were eggs, or scruffy grey balls of fluff – gull chicks.

The racket never stopped. It was deafening. They screeched like banshees, yapped like dogs. Sometimes they clicked with their beaks.

"Ka ka ka!" Their harsh warning calls sounded constantly.

Then there were softer, more tender sounds. *"Klioo,"* when they greeted their mates. Or *"Mew, mew,"* like a cat when they fed their young.

They made so many different sounds it wasn't hard to believe that they had their own, gull language.

But it was only gull voices you heard in Mackenzie Point. Were there any humans alive down there in the town streets? If there were, you couldn't tell. They must be creeping about, making no noise at all.

On the top of the gothic turret of the Town Hall sat one lone gull. He was huge, with pure white feathers and a brutal hatchet beak. Like an emperor, Red Eye surveyed his town, watched the movements of his gull subjects and their human slaves.

All seemed well. Out on the rocky shore, teams

of slaves shuffled about. They were the entire population of Mackenzie Point, about three hundred in all. From dawn until dusk they collected food for the gulls. They dug up lugworms, collected starfish and crabs, prised shellfish off rocks. The Creepers stood by, to make sure they didn't slacken. But it wasn't only the Creepers who kept them in line.

A man was working, collecting limpets, with his small son beside him.

The man straightened up for a second, rubbing his painful back.

Instantly, Snapper swooped down, pecking at his head, making an attack noise, *"Agh, agh, agh!"* Hook Beak joined in, screeching. Red Eye's bodyguard were skuas, the most aggressive of seabirds.

The man slumped onto the sand, his head bleeding. But the skuas didn't stop there. They were diving for his son now. The little boy screamed in terror, tried to cover his head.

"No!" begged the man. "Punish me. Not him!"

He staggered to his feet and carried on feverishly collecting food. Only then did the skuas back off. No one else looked up. They all worked twice as fast.

"*Kwarrr!*" Red Eye screamed his victory call, stamped his clawed feet, beat his great wings. It pleased him to see the humans so obedient.

Red Eye was a one-off, the result of a strange set of circumstances. He was albino for a start, that made him special. But his extra intelligence came from somewhere else.

He was just an embryo inside his egg when it happened, in a nest on the old iron fort. Many gulls raised their chicks there, before it got demolished. They nested on any metal ledge they could find. But Red Eye's parents had, by chance, made their nest inside an old rubber lifebelt.

One night, there was a massive electrical storm. Right over the fort, black clouds gathered. Lightning sizzled down and struck the fort, again and again. People from Mackenzie Point saw it, lit up in a spooky blue glow. They saw electric flashes chasing all over it and smelled the sulphur a kilometre away.

Most of the gulls flew off. Those that didn't were fried, along with all the eggs and little chicks. Even the conger eels that swam around the fort's iron legs got electrocuted. Only Red Eye, inside his egg, insulated by the rubber ring, survived. But the electrical surge had done weird things to his developing brain. It grew in unnatural ways. So, when Red Eye finally hatched, he was a monster, a freak, with a brain much too smart for his bird body.

"Kwarrr!" shrieked Red Eye again, just to let everyone down there know he was boss.

A man and a woman crossed the square. Both had shaved off their hair. On top of their smooth, bald heads they'd drawn a great eye – in red marker pen. That red eye badge showed they were Creepers, humans loyal to the gulls. It could be seen from above, so the gulls didn't mistake them for mere slaves, and swoop down to attack them.

They were carrying something. Baskets of glittering fish – it was Red Eye's dinner.

Only Creepers could take out boats and fish. Red Eye knew they wouldn't try to escape. The Creepers had privileges. The other slaves lived locked in the school, when they weren't working. But the Creepers had the pick of the houses, the best food. And, most of all, the gulls let them live.

The Creepers placed the fish on the ground, like an offering. Then they backed swiftly away, with heads bowed. Red Eye didn't swoop down to eat immediately. He knew no other gull would dare touch what was his.

Not the fish, nor the other glittering thing that lay on the ledge beside him. It was the chain that had once belonged to the Mayor of Mackenzie Point – the foolish human who'd tried to shoot him.

It was made up of big gold medallions that flashed like mirrors. Red Eye gazed into one of them. His own reflection stared back. If Prof. Talltrees had seen what happened next he would have been horrified. He would have pulled out his team straight away. Because Red Eye didn't attack his reflection. Instead, he jutted his neck out proudly, and began preening himself. He knew exactly who he was looking at. The King of Mackenzie Point, that's who.

Another gull landed on a ledge nearby. Red Eye's neck whipped round. His killer shark eyes gleamed. He let out a savage scream: *"Ka, ka, ka!"*

The smaller gull instantly made submissive gestures, keeping its head ducked low, not making eye contact.

It mewed, like a cat. *"Mew, mew."*

That meant, "Don't hurt me."

Red Eye stopped being threatening, let it approach.

The other gull was ringed, with a black band. It was Danny's pet, the gull who'd been brought up with humans. It had seen Danny get off the train at Clayborough with two other humans. Then it had flown straight back to Mackenzie Point.

The two gulls touched beaks. They began making sounds: clicks, croaks, yaps, low melodious "*klioows*". What were they communicating? Was Jet betraying Danny? Only someone with Meriel's powers could tell.

Chapter Five

"No," said Danny, "no torches."

They were walking along the causeway out to Mackenzie Point. It was getting very dark.

"They might see the light," Danny explained.

Ellis shrugged okay and switched off the torch he'd just taken out of his backpack.

"They mostly don't attack at night," said Danny, gnawing on his fingernails. "Mostly."

The gulls didn't have good night vision. Unless they had lights to guide them. And then they'd come screaming down out of a black night sky, claws ready to rake, hatchet beaks ready to rip.

Sometimes moonlight was enough. Danny checked the sky. They were safe, for the moment. Clouds covered the moon.

Danny shuddered. He pulled on his battered old bike helmet, just in case.

Ellis thought, *He's a nervous wreck!* Danny twitched at every odd sound. His eyes flickered this way and that. Not that there was much to see. Just the white gravel track under their feet. But from the blackness beyond came the *shushing* of waves, the smell of rotting seaweed.

Ellis didn't feel they were in danger. So his senses weren't on red alert. But he was still picking up all sorts of odd details the others missed. He did it automatically.

Up close, he heard mice squeaking through the seagrass, the whirr of a hawk moth's wings. Then, from far away out at sea, came another sound. A sort of blooping *whoosh*. Ellis grinned. It was a hump-backed whale who'd come to the surface to breathe. He waited. There it came, drifting in with the wind, the foul stink of the air it blew out, along with the water. Hump-backed whales have really bad breath.

"There's no foxes," said Ellis.

He'd been expecting foxes, hunting rabbits through the dunes. Foxes smelled bad too, with a sort of musky stink, but not as bad as hump-backed whales.

"Gulls scared off the foxes," muttered Danny. Then, "Keep to the causeway," he whispered in a worried voice. "There are mudflats out there. If you get stuck in the mud and the tide comes in..."

"Yeah, yeah, you already told us," said Meriel. She sounded irritable.

Ellis knew how she felt. They'd been scrunching along this narrow strip of land, with the sea on both sides, for what seemed like for ever.

"So where is this place Mackenzie Point?" asked Ellis. "Does it really exist?"

"*Shhhh!*" begged Danny.

With any luck, the gulls would be roosting now. But there could be Creepers about. After dark, they prowled around Mackenzie Point like policemen, to make sure no one tried to escape. The only way you could get out was by walking, like Danny did. Vehicles were useless. You couldn't drive them along this crumbling causeway. And all boats had been destroyed. Except for a few the Creepers used to catch Red Eye's dinner.

"Please, keep your voices down," Danny whispered.

For heaven's sake, thought Ellis. *Is this kid paranoid or what?*

Like Meriel, he still couldn't decide about this mission. Could Danny, for some weird reasons of his own, be lying? When it got light, perhaps all they'd see was some peaceful little seaside town, with maybe a few gulls, nicking people's chips.

I'm going to be really mad, thought Ellis, *if I've walked all this way for nothing.*

And Meriel would be even madder, if she couldn't meet this brainy bird. What was his name, Red Eye?

"You believe in all this?" he murmured to Meriel.

She'd been silent throughout most of their walk. Was she in a trance, doing her mind-reading thing with animals? But she preferred to see the animals to do that. And you couldn't see anything in this darkness. So maybe she was just being unsociable. Meriel never chatted just to be polite.

"Well, do you?" he insisted.

Meriel still didn't answer. Something freaky was happening inside her head. She was seeing pictures. She thought in pictures, not words, most of the time, like animals do. But these pictures weren't of her own making. She saw gulls flying, skimming across silvery wave tops, floating on the breeze like white butterflies. They were beautiful pictures. But where did they come from? How did they get inside her brain? They got brighter, more vivid, the closer they got to their journey's end. And they caused a strange, longing ache in her heart.

At last they were off the causeway. Now they were walking on grass.

"We're here," said Danny. "This is Mackenzie Point."

"Wait!" said Ellis suddenly.

He stopped dead in his tracks. He'd heard something he didn't expect. Seaweed popping, from out of the dark somewhere. To his extra-sharp ears it sounded as loud as gunfire. There it went again, *pop, pop, pop.* It would take a heavy tread to do that – a human, for sure.

"There's someone out there," hissed Ellis, jerking his head to the right.

"Creeper!" squeaked Danny. He dived into the long grass. And just vanished.

"Where's he gone?" said Meriel. Ellis shrugged. But then, as if from a grave, a hand reached up and grabbed his ankle.

"I'm down here," hissed Danny.

Meriel kneeled down, parted the tough razor grass. There was a dark hole. Some kind of hiding place?

"Hurry!" a voice echoed, from somewhere at the bottom.

"Can we get through there?" asked Ellis. It seemed like a tight fit.

But Meriel wriggled in, feet first, and disappeared.

Ellis hesitated, looked around, listened. He couldn't hear the seaweed popping now. Or any other suspicious sounds. Whoever it was had moved away. Did they need to take cover? But there was something about Danny's scared voice, this spooky place. Ellis felt the hairs lifting on the back of his neck. He was used to being alone in the night, tracking animals. But somehow, he didn't want to be alone out here. He put his backpack through first. Heard it drop with a soft thud. Then he squeezed through the hole after Meriel.

"Whoa!" He dropped down, then sprawled onto soft sand.

Scrambling up, he switched on his torch. He ignored Danny's panicky voice – "They might see it from up there!" – and flashed the beam around.

"Wow!" he said. "What is this place?"

Low tunnels led off in all directions.

"Is it a mine or something?" asked Meriel. She was paying attention again. Those mind pictures, of swooping, soaring gulls, had gone as soon as they came underground. And so had that strange, wistful yearning.

"No." Danny shook his head, as they crept along a tunnel, stooping low so they didn't bang their heads. "It's not a mine. It's from the war. There were loads of big guns on Mackenzie Point. So soldiers could shoot at enemy planes. These tunnels connected the gun emplacements. We hide here from the gulls and the Creepers."

"Who's *we*?" asked Ellis.

"Me and this other kid, TJ. The proper entrance was blocked up ages ago. It's supposed to be dangerous down here. But me and TJ, we know secret ways in."

Ellis had a hundred questions to ask. But Danny was already scurrying ahead. He seemed more confident now he was underground. As if, for the time being at least, he felt safe. He called back over his shoulder. "I'll take you to meet TJ!"

Chapter Six

Danny led them through the brick-lined tunnels. He seemed to know this place like the back of his hand.

"Me and TJ played down here when we were little," he explained. "It was our big secret. No one knew we'd found a way in."

The tunnel opened out into a cave-like space, the roof propped up by wooden beams.

"This is our den," said Danny proudly. "This is where me and TJ hide out."

Ellis switched off his torch to save the batteries. There was light here already from a smoky yellow candle flame. And stuff piled around: sleeping bags, clothes, all sorts of junk.

"TJ!" Danny shouted. His voice echoed down the dark tunnels. "TJ! TJ!" But there was no reply. Danny looked anxious. "TJ should be here!" he said. "He never goes anywhere without his armour."

"Armour?" said Meriel. All she could see was a pile of metal scrap: tin trays, a car hubcap, an old wartime helmet.

"Or his baseball bat," said Danny, picking it up.

"What's he want that for?" asked Meriel.

"To fight off gulls with," said Danny.

"*Huh!*" snorted Meriel, scornfully. "A baseball bat? Fat lot of use that'd be!"

"Well, it's better than nothing," muttered Danny.

Better than umbrellas. His mind flashed back to the beginning. In the beginning, after the gulls invaded, people in Mackenzie Point had gone out with their umbrellas up.

Umbrellas! thought Danny, with a sad shake of his head.

They'd really thought those brollies could protect them. There were big stripy beach ones, candy-pink plastic ones. The whole town went out under brollies. It would have been funny if it hadn't been so tragic. The gulls had dived down, ripped those brollies to shreds...

His mind snapped back to the present: "TJ should be here," he said again.

He started running around, searching, one second in the candle glow, the next racing off into darkness. He came back, his face creased with worry. "TJ isn't here," he said. "Something's wrong."

Meriel shrugged. "Maybe he's just gone out for a bit."

"What, with the Creepers out there! And those psycho gulls!" Danny yelled at her, distraught.

"Look, calm down," said Ellis.

"You just don't understand," said Danny, despairing. "You think this is all a big joke, don't you?"

"Here, have something to eat," said Ellis. "I brought sandwiches." He rummaged around in his backpack. "Banana or peanut butter?"

"I don't care," said Danny, snatching one and wolfing it down.

Any sandwich was a luxury. He and TJ went on food raids, stealing from gardens or houses. But sometimes all they got was carrots or turnips to gnaw. Or shellfish from the rock pools. They were disgusting, like eating slugs, but they kept you alive.

Suddenly Ellis said, "There are cats down here." He was crouching down, tracing paw prints in the sandy floor with his finger.

"I know," said Meriel. "They're watching us now." She nodded to the right. In the distance, in the blackness at the end of a tunnel, were four pairs of gleaming eyes.

"There's one big one, with really big paw prints," said Ellis. "Think you can read their minds?"

Meriel shrugged. "Don't know." She got up and wandered off.

Danny stopped chewing his sandwich, gazed after her. What was that conversation all about? Meriel was so creepy. And that look in her eyes, that proud defiant stare, as if she didn't care about anyone or anything. He wished again that Prof. Talltrees had come, instead of these two.

Ellis was asking him, "Where did the cats come from?"

"From Wonderland," said Danny. "My granddad kept them to catch the rats. They came down here with me, to hide from the gulls."

Gulls killed cats whenever they could. But these cats were half-wild anyway, even when Granddad kept them. They helped keep him and TJ alive too. When they went out hunting at night, they brought rats back. Roasted rat didn't taste too bad, once you got used to it.

"Your granddad owns Wonderland?" asked Ellis. He realized that Danny had hardly said anything personal about himself, or his family. "Where is he? Is he still there? Is he a Creeper?"

Danny shook his head violently, spitting out sandwich crumbs. "No way!" he said, insulted. "Granddad wouldn't be a Creeper. He tried to fight the gulls! Remember I told you about the guy that fell off a ladder?"

Ellis nodded.

"Well, that was my granddad," said Danny.

When the first gulls flew in and nested on Wonderland's roof, Granddad had thought he could stop them. He'd climbed up to the roof with a rake. They'd gone berserk, flying round his head shrieking and clawing. He'd lost his footing and fallen. He'd been taken by boat to the mainland. Danny would never forget that moment when he heard the clatter, ran outside and saw Granddad all crumpled up on the ground. He'd thought he was dead.

"He's in hospital in Clayborough," said Danny. "He's been there for over a month. It was a bad fall. He doesn't know about any of this, about the gulls taking over – I mean, it all happened so quick. He thinks he fell by accident. He didn't though."

"Won't he wonder why you're not visiting?" asked Ellis.

"No," Danny replied. "He said not to. He said it was my job to stay here, look after Wonderland for him." Danny gave a bitter little laugh. "He'd go ballistic, if he could see it now."

Not that it was much to look at, even before the gulls came. Wonderland had been closed for ages, its helter-skelter and roller coaster and Big Wheel falling down. But Granddad still kept the old machines going – the claw that grabbed prizes and the pinball. Even though nobody ever came to play them.

"That's why the gulls are after me," added Danny. "'Cos Granddad raked their nests. That's why I hid down here."

"But what about your parents?" asked Ellis.

"I live with Granddad now," said Danny, as if that was all Ellis needed to know. Then he added, "My mum's travelling…"

She was off round the world with her new boyfriend on his motorbike. Danny didn't mind, he was cool about that. His granddad had practically brought him up, since his dad left, before he was born. Danny loved his granddad – and his mum. When he was little he'd thought everyone's mum was like his. Going off travelling, working abroad, sending postcards from faraway places. Danny had a whole collection of them, stuck up on his bedroom wall.

"Where's TJ?" fretted Danny. "He should be here."

His voice was slurred with weariness. His eyelids kept closing. He had too much to worry about to go to sleep. "I've got to stay awake," he told himself. "Wait for TJ."

"Who is TJ anyhow?" asked Ellis.

"You know I told you about the Mayor that disappeared?"

"Yeah."

"Well, TJ is his son. The gulls are after him too, because of what his dad did. His dad tried to shoot Red Eye, but he missed – I told you, didn't I? I..."

Danny's voice trailed away.

Ellis watched, as Danny's head slumped onto his knees. He'd fallen asleep.

Ellis took a swig of the drink he'd packed. Then stretched himself out on a sleeping bag. He still didn't know how much of all this to believe. A tracker only trusted the evidence of his own eyes. But when tomorrow came he'd see for himself what was happening at Mackenzie Point.

In the tunnels, Meriel had found a cat. She'd got the torch with her. She switched it on, laid it on the ground so it didn't dazzle either of them.

"Hello, kitty," said Meriel.

It was a big ginger tomcat. He was bruised and battered with half an ear torn off. He looked like he'd spent his life fighting.

Meriel wasn't in the mood for mind-reading, for

going into a trance. That really drained her and she was too tired tonight.

But she didn't need to read his mind to see this cat was scared. His eyes, in the torchlight, were white and terrified. His fur was on end. He spat at her, "*PSSSST!*" He backed off, his back arched, disappeared into darkness.

"What's wrong with you?" Meriel called after him. "I'm not a gull!"

But then, an image came slamming into her head. Meriel thought, *What's going on?* She was used to going into animals' minds. But it was when *she* wanted – it was her choice. Now something, uninvited, was invading her brain. And she had terrible suspicions about what it was, which grew stronger with each invasion.

This time, she was looking down from a high-up place. A strange tower-like place, like something out of a fairy tale, with four stone dragons, one crouching at each corner. The town spread below her, the wind ruffled her feathers. She felt her own power. She was King of the World! She spread out white, feathery bird's wings...

"No!" said Meriel fiercely. "Get out of my head!"

With a superhuman effort she blocked out the scary, seductive pictures.

"And stay out," she whispered, as she crept back down the tunnel.

"Danny's asleep," said Ellis, as she came back into the den. He offered her the can of drink. "Want some?"

She took a gulp. Ellis said, "Are you all right?" Her face was white, as if she'd just had a big shock.

"Course I'm all right," snapped Meriel.

"Okay, okay," said Ellis. "Don't bite my head off. Only asking."

A serious look came onto his face. "Do you think there's anything in this Red Eye stuff?" he asked Meriel. "Danny seems scared stiff of him. He says the whole town is. I mean, how can one seagull have that much power?"

"Well, he can't, can he? It's just stupid," said Meriel. She wrapped herself up in the other sleeping bag, turned her back and, apparently, went to sleep.

The candle spluttered out. Ellis lay in darkness. He didn't like it down here. He hated cramped, small places. They gave him the creeps – he felt he was suffocating. Like he'd been buried alive. He'd much rather be in the open air.

He knew Meriel wasn't like him. She felt at home in tunnels. She often went inside the mind of Travis, her weasel, to experience his world. Weasels squeeze through the tiniest spaces, hunting mice and rabbits.

Ellis closed his eyes, so he couldn't see the tunnel roof, which seemed to be pressing down on him like a coffin lid.

His mind drifted back to his parents. They'd run a nature reserve in Africa. It was there he'd learned his tracking skills, going off for days with Gift, the best tracker in the district.

They'd tracked pythons through the bush and seen them swimming, twisted together in a waterhole. They'd tracked down a missing baby girl, once. She'd been carried off by hyenas and they'd found her, alive, in a nest of puppies. Ellis smiled at those good memories. Then the darker ones came – they always did. Of that time, two years ago, when he and Gift came back home at dawn and found the electric fence broken down. Gift had gone ahead into the house. Then come out and told Ellis, "Don't go inside." Ellis had disappeared into the bush for days. When he'd returned, ragged and starving, he'd found Prof. Talltrees waiting for him – a tall lanky guy with a bad limp, and an eyepatch on his scarred face.

The Prof was an old friend of his parents. He'd spent months at their nature reserve, studying wild dogs. But that had been years ago, when Ellis was just a baby. Ellis knew his parents admired the Prof. They talked about him often. But Ellis never knew that they'd named him, in their will, as his guardian.

Never even knew they'd made a will, Ellis thought to himself, lying in the dark. *They never told me*. But it would have freaked him out if they *had* told him. Like they knew those poachers would get them in the end.

Ellis had a photo in his jacket pocket – he carried it everywhere – of his mum, tanned and smiling, feeding a lion cub a bottle of milk. A baby lion whose parents had both been killed by poachers too.

Stop it! Ellis told his brain. He tried not to think about the past too much. It was too painful.

He thought about Meriel instead. She'd been there, with the Prof, when he'd stumbled back half-crazy from his days in the bush, mourning his parents. He'd felt a bond with her, because she'd lost her family too.

That was the first time I saw her mind read, Ellis thought. *In Africa.* He smiled in the dark as he remembered.

White-Face, a big, old, bad-tempered baboon on the reserve, had come charging up to Ellis, screaming and showing his yellow teeth. Ellis had been going to run. "He's only showing off," Meriel had told him, in that cool voice of hers. "He won't hurt you."

"How d'you know that?" Ellis had demanded.

"Because I just went inside his head," she'd answered.

"Can you do that with people?" he'd once asked her. "Read their minds?" It had worried him – no one had the right to read his private thoughts.

But she'd said, "No. It's simple with animals. People's minds are too messy."

Lying there in the sleeping bag, Ellis let out a long sigh. Sometimes Meriel amazed him. He didn't believe in magic. He only believed what he saw with his own eyes. But Meriel was a mystery, you had to admit it, and more than a little freaky. Sometimes she irritated him half to death. She wasn't the easiest person in the world to get on with. Sometimes, she was downright unfriendly.

And what about *her* past? How did the Prof get to be *her* guardian? That was a mystery too – neither the Prof nor Meriel ever talked about it. But there was some deep connection between them, anyone could see that. For a start, she'd been with the Prof much longer than he had. And Ellis knew the Prof's injuries were something to do with Meriel.

But that was all Ellis knew. Sometimes he'd even wondered if the Prof was Meriel's father.

Naah, he'd decided. *You're probably wrong about that*. Meriel didn't seem to love the Prof, not like Ellis had loved his own dad. But then she didn't love anyone, not people anyway.

Go to sleep, Ellis told himself, yawning. It was pointless tormenting himself with all these questions. He'd find out some day. When the Prof or Meriel decided to tell him.

And, besides, he needed some rest. It was going to be a big day tomorrow. He and Meriel were finally going to find out the truth about Red Eye.

Chapter Seven

Someone was shaking him awake, yelling in his ear.

"Gerroff," said Ellis, rolling over. "I'm asleep."

Then he remembered where he was. Not at home in the city museum but at Mackenzie Point, on a mission. He sat bolt upright. Meriel was shaking him.

"He's gone," she said. "Danny's gone."

"Where?"

"Dunno. But he's taken the armour," said Meriel. "And TJ's baseball bat. I bet he's gone looking for TJ."

"Come on," said Ellis. "We've got to go after him."

They didn't need the torch now. The tunnels were gloomy but not pitch black. Light filtered down here and there through rusty ventilation grills.

"This is where we came in," said Ellis. He knew that absolutely. Wherever they go, trackers always map out the way in their minds, so they can be certain to find their way back.

Meriel glanced up at the crack they'd wriggled through. Pink light came flooding in.

"It's dawn," said Ellis.

"We should take some protection," said Meriel, "against the gulls."

"There's no time for that," said Ellis, surprised she should be so cautious. That wasn't like Meriel at all. Usually, she never gave a thought to safety.

And he still wasn't totally convinced by Danny's story. How could seagulls make you so scared?

What can they really *do*, Ellis thought, *besides dump on you from a great height?*

He'd have liked to know if Meriel was convinced. But she wasn't giving much away. She seemed even more distant than usual on this mission, as if something was troubling her. But he didn't have time for that now. Danny was out there, on his own, with only a baseball bat to defend himself. Plus, Danny was scared. Scared people do stupid things.

Ellis climbed out of the tunnels, followed by Meriel. They were standing on a grassy cliff top.

"*Wow!*" said Ellis. It was his first glimpse of Mackenzie Point in daylight.

Sea and mudflats, stained red by the fiery dawn sky, surrounded the little headland. To his left the causeway snaked off into the hazy distance. To his right, across the dunes, was the town – a cluster of shabby buildings round the Town Hall. The Town Hall seemed far too big and grand for such a run-down little dump. It had been built in Victorian times when Mackenzie Point was a bustling and important place.

Ellis saw no people, all the streets were deserted. But was that Wonderland, that Danny's granddad owned? It looked like a whole lot of giant, iced wedding cakes, with the Big Wheel, roller coaster and all the other rides hidden by thick layers of white gull guano.

But where were the gulls? Hadn't Danny said there were thousands of them?

Knew *he was making this up*, thought Ellis.

But then Meriel said, "There's Danny!"

Ellis saw him too, further along the cliff tops. He wasn't looking in their direction, but staring out to sea. He was waving TJ's baseball bat around.

For heaven's sake, thought Ellis. *What* does *he look like?*

In his anti-gull armour he was a weird, fantastic figure. A cross between a medieval knight and a robot kid, clumsily made out of scrap metal. He had his World War Two helmet on. Car hubcaps were strapped to his chest and back like breastplates. They gleamed like silver suns. And what was that tied round his legs and arms? Bits of guttering pipe?

When Ellis ran up to meet Danny, he was laughing. But when he saw Danny's face, he stopped dead. It was a mask of horror. Danny was pointing a metal arm, gibbering, "It's TJ! They've got him!"

"Where? Where?" said Ellis.

In the bay below all he could see was gulls. A great, swooping, swirling, screaming mass of herring and black-headed gulls. It looked like the entire colony was out there.

And it seemed like they were mobbing something. The mass was moving, further out over the mudflats. And beyond, Ellis could see the sea pouring into the bay, flashing like fire in the rising sun. It was roaring in, very fast.

"Where's TJ?" said Ellis again.

Then the gulls parted. And for a moment, he saw a tiny staggering figure, flapping its arms wildly about. Then the screeching gull pack, like a great evil white cloud, closed again over its head.

"Get down!" said Ellis. Meriel and he flattened themselves into the long grass. He dragged Danny down. But the gulls weren't paying *them* any attention. They were too busy with TJ.

"They're driving him out onto the mudflats!" said Danny. "He'll get stuck. He'll drown!"

It was happening just like Danny said. The great gull pack was breaking up, wheeling away. Their work was done. And now there was just a tiny figure, alone in the middle of the bay. It struggled. But it seemed to be stuck in the mud. And the tide was speeding in like a bullet train.

"We have to help him," said Ellis.

"We can't," said Meriel, bluntly. "Look."

Ellis hadn't seen them before, he'd been concentrating on TJ. But, on the cliff tops overlooking the bay, there were people, lined up in a row. They were some of Red Eye's human slaves, brought out to watch TJ's punishment. Gulls were hovering above them. But the slaves were silent, heads bowed. Some, with shiny shaved scalps, patrolled the row of slaves like prison guards. The gulls left the guards alone.

"Look at their heads," said Ellis. "They've drawn eyes on them!"

"Creepers," whispered Danny.

It made his skin crawl, those red, staring eyes, like the wadjet eyes in Ancient Egyptian wall paintings. From above, the Creepers must look like one-eyed monsters.

"Why don't they *do* something?" said Ellis, shocked. "They're just standing there, watching."

But he could answer his own question. Hadn't Danny said the Creepers were loyal to the gulls?

And the others, the people of Mackenzie Point, were too afraid.

"I *knew* they'd get TJ," sobbed Danny, distraught.

They'd already got his dad, the Mayor – Danny had no doubts about that. Maybe driven him out onto the mudflats, drowned him, just like this. And when the gulls punished someone, they didn't stop there. They punished whole families. It was a very good way of controlling people. No one dared rebel, once they'd learned their family would suffer too. But there was one member of the Mayor's family the gulls wouldn't be punishing.

"See that Creeper?" said Danny, raising a trembling arm. "The one at the end? That's TJ's big brother."

Ellis wasn't sure which one Danny was pointing to. But he said: "What? You're kidding! He's just standing there doing nothing? While his own brother drowns?"

"Huh!" said Meriel, as if it was all you could expect of humans. But she was thinking, *You're clever, Red Eye.* He ruled through fear. But he was cunning too. He split families, made them betray each other.

Danny leaped up. "I'm going to get TJ!"

"No!" hissed Ellis, pulling him down.

With the Creepers watching and the gulls, it would be suicide.

"I'll get those gulls if they try to stop me!" raved Danny.

But the sea was sneaking ever closer to TJ. He was yelling out something. His voice carried over the bay. Was it, "Help me!"?

But the watchers on the cliff top, including his Creeper brother, just stood there, waiting for the sea to come in.

"I'm going!" said Danny.

He started crawling towards the steep cliff path that led down to the bay. His scrap-metal armour clanked and rattled.

"No, wait," said Ellis.

Something else was rushing in too, with the tide. It was a thick white fog, a sea fret. It came pouring over the far horizon, moving faster than the tide. Soon it would fill the whole bay. No one would be able to see a thing.

As if she could read Ellis's mind, Meriel said, "Gulls don't fly in fog."

"You stay here," said Ellis. "Look after Danny." He shot a look at Meriel that said, *I don't want him doing anything stupid*.

Meriel didn't usually take orders, not even from the Prof. But this time, she agreed. "Okay."

"What's going on?" said Danny. "You two are just *talking*! And TJ's drowning out there!"

"No, he's not," said Ellis. "I'm going to get him."

Chapter Eight

Ellis was shut in by fog. It muffled sounds. He could see his hand, if he stretched out his arm. But not much further. Fog writhed and twisted in ghostly shapes all around him.

He wasn't lost though. Before the fog had moved in, before he'd gone scrambling down the steep cliff path, he'd mapped out the bay in his head. It seemed like one vast expanse of mud. But he'd seen channels cutting through the mud, banks of shells.

He was crunching across some shells now. He wasn't worried about the gulls or the Creepers. He knew he was invisible from above.

He didn't even need the map in his head. Because he could track TJ across the mudflats. TJ had trainers, with stars on the soles. You could see by his footprints that he'd been in a panic. He'd blundered all over the place as he was driven, buffeted by gulls' wings, towards the sea. Sometimes, the gulls had wheeled down so low that Ellis could see the feathery scrapes their wing tips had made in the mud.

Then TJ started yelling out again, "Help! Help!" in a voice hoarse with shouting. Ellis headed towards those desperate cries.

He looked down. Salty water was sneaking in, sloshing over his trainers. It was the first ripples of sea, before the big waves came.

Better find TJ fast, he thought.

And here he was. Ellis almost bumped into him. TJ was a skinny little kid with wild eyes and a face grey with shock. He grabbed Ellis's arm and wouldn't let go. "Help me!"

"I'm going to," said Ellis. "Danny sent me. Just stop struggling."

TJ's shoes had already sunk into the mud. Now he was dragging Ellis in too. Ellis could feel himself being sucked down.

"Stand still," said Ellis. "Or we'll both drown."

With his arms clenched round TJ's waist, he tried hauling him out of the mud. At first it wouldn't let him go. Then, with a great *slurp*, TJ was free, falling forward into a salty channel.

"Come on!" said Ellis.

The sea was rumbling somewhere very close, like a great big engine. Water was swirling in now, gurgling round their ankles.

But the fog was getting denser. They were in thick white cloud. It was like being lost in the sky. Ellis knew he was going to need all his tracking skills to get them out of this.

And TJ was already stumbling the wrong way.

Ellis reached out, grabbed a fistful of fog. He had to run after him. "No!" he yelled, dragging TJ back. "You're running out to sea. It's this way."

"How do you know?" screamed TJ, right in his face.

"Look for the signs," said Ellis. "Look at the way the water's flowing."

But Ellis was scared too. He could hear his own heart echoing, *boom, boom, boom*. He was breathing much too fast. For a few steps they followed water rushing in. Then the channel ended.

Where now? thought Ellis.

The roaring sea was behind them. But which way to the shore? He turned – a wall of fog. He turned again – another white wall. For a second his sense of direction deserted him. Somewhere above this fog was sun. But down here it was cold; he was already chilled to the bone.

"Which way?" TJ was pleading.

Then Ellis felt a breeze on his cheek, coming from the land. He turned towards it. "That way!" he said.

Glug, went the mud as he pulled his feet free.

Now there were other signs too. He could smell coconut, drifting through the fog. Yellow gorse flowers smell like coconut. And there'd been gorse bushes on the cliff top.

He hurried on, with TJ scurrying after.

They sloshed through water, then stopped,

sliding on mud. Ellis crouched down. There were footprints, only just made, of wellington boots. Size twelve, bigger feet than the Prof's. Who was out here, blundering round in the fog?

He called out, "Hey? Anyone there?" But no one answered. It seemed they were on their own.

"Are we going the right way?" TJ panted, sticking as close to him as his shadow.

Ellis stared ahead. But it was hopeless. It just made his eyes ache. He couldn't see a thing through the fog.

He had to depend on the signs. But he'd lost the coconut scent.

We could be going round in circles, he thought. And that sea was coming in horribly fast, filling the channels around them with deep, foamy water.

Up on the cliff top, Meriel and Danny were hidden in the long grass. The bay was below them, like a giant soup bowl filled with fog. It was even drifting up to the cliff tops now, in a swirling white mist.

The Creepers had led the people away. There was nothing to see, now the fog filled the bay. The slaves looked like a chain gang shuffling along. But there was no need to shackle their ankles. They were too beaten down and crushed to even think of escape, or resistance.

The gulls had gone back to their roosts. Soon the sun would rise higher and burn off the fog. And then they'd be out and about, swooping over the town. They'd shriek and squabble and fight amongst themselves. But Red Eye saw everything from his high tower. And, if they went too far, his bodyguard of vicious skuas would swoop down to attack them too. Just like they did the human slaves.

Meriel stared down into the bay. It looked as if it was packed tight with clouds. You couldn't see a thing.

"Hope Ellis is okay," she said, biting her lip.

Danny was worried sick too. But he stared at her, surprised. Her voice, usually cool and indifferent, sounded anxious. So she cared about Ellis, did she?

Then she corrected herself, scolding herself as if Danny wasn't there. "Why are you worrying? Course he's okay." Ellis had tracked himself out of trickier situations than this.

But it seemed like she needed her mind taking off what was happening, down in the bay.

"Tell me about TJ," she ordered Danny.

"There's not much to tell," said Danny. "He's just like me, an ordinary kid. Except, it's crazy, the gulls going after him because of his dad. Because TJ was scared of his dad. His dad was a great big bully. And his big brother's mean too. That's why he became a Creeper. Those Creepers are all bullies and sneaks and cowards!"

"Maybe they're just scared," said Meriel. "Everybody gets scared."

"Yeah, but they don't become Creepers!" said Danny.

Meriel shrugged. People were a mystery to her. Their minds were far too complicated. She understood animals much better.

Danny chewed on his knuckles. "What's happening down there?" he fretted, staring into the fog.

Down in the bay, Ellis was in trouble. He depended on his senses to track. But the fog made him blind and muffled sounds.

He didn't want to admit it to TJ. His pride would hardly let him admit it to himself. But, *You're lost*, his brain whispered. Lost, in a spooky, white candyfloss world.

His legs felt heavy. Every step, he had to haul his feet out of the mud. And he was so cold, beyond shivering. He could feel his lips turning blue.

TJ was practically collapsing. He'd already been through a terrible trauma, mobbed, then left to drown by the gulls.

"Don't sit down!" said Ellis, urgently. TJ looked like he just wanted to sprawl on the mud and fall asleep. "Keep awake!" said Ellis, shaking him.

TJ staggered on. He tried to climb a sandbank. It crumbled like cake beneath him. He slid to the bottom and stayed there, a helpless heap.

"No," said Ellis, hauling him up. He'd seen something. The seaweed had been red before. But now he'd found brown seaweed on a rock. He crouched down, to look.

He felt hope fizzing in his heart, like bubbles. "It's okay!" he told TJ. "We're heading in the right direction."

Ellis had noticed it before the fog rolled in, when he'd surveyed the bay with a tracker's eye. On Mackenzie Point red seaweed grew near deep water. But brown seaweed grew further up the shore, near dry land.

Look for more brown seaweed! Ellis ordered his brain. He just had to keep cool now. Not get frantic again.

Then he saw it, even more brown seaweed on the rocks.

"This way!" he told TJ, plunging into the fog.

And he knew he was right, because they'd stopped squelching through water. The ground was firmer under their feet.

And there was another kind of seaweed now, brown twisted ribbons called channel wrack, which grew even higher up the shore. And so they trudged on, following the seaweed to safety.

And now they were scrunching on shells, then sand. Ellis almost fell over an old oil drum washed up on the beach.

"We're back!" he told TJ. He recognized that drum. The path up the cliff was right beside it.

When Ellis and TJ appeared, shivering and muddy, at the top of the cliff, Meriel didn't make a fuss. But when she said, "What took you so long?" Ellis knew she'd been worried.

The fog on the cliff top was burning off. You could see the sun now, a lemon smudge through the smoky haze.

"We'd better get back underground," said Ellis.

Soon the gulls would be flying out on patrol and Creepers prowling about.

Danny couldn't speak at first. He was thrilled beyond words to see TJ safe. He just had a huge sloppy grin on his face. Then he gave TJ a couple of friendly cuffs. "Have you got belly button fluff for brains?" he asked his friend. "What did you go out there for? In daylight? Without your armour and baseball bat?"

Meriel didn't hear TJ's reply, as Ellis was hustling him and Danny back into the tunnels. "Come on, we can't hang around up here."

She was alone on the cliff top now. She was about to dive underground too when, suddenly, out of the fog behind her, came the clicking of beaks. And a soft call: *"Klioo!"*

Meriel's head whipped round.

At first, she couldn't see anything. Then she saw two dark shapes in the mist. The fog swirled away. And revealed a monster gull with pure white feathers and glittering ruby eyes.

"Red Eye!" breathed Meriel. Who else could it be?

There was another, smaller gull with him, with a black leg ring. But Meriel barely noticed. She had eyes only for Red Eye.

He stared at her – lordly, cruel and completely unafraid.

The Prof had told Meriel once that birds evolved from small dinosaurs. And she could see that in Red Eye. His scaly claws, his snake-like neck, his flat head – he was basically a velociraptor. Except his eyes weren't dinosaur eyes. They shone with an intelligence that was almost human.

He opened his yellow beak. The inside wasn't yellow. It was a shocking bright crimson, like fresh blood.

"*Kwarr!*" he screeched at her, tossing his sleek, feathery head in triumph.

Meriel had suspected it before. But now she suddenly knew it, for certain. It was Red Eye who'd invaded her brain in the tunnels. He'd been doing it ever since she'd set foot on Mackenzie Point.

A shudder convulsed her body. She couldn't help it. There was a sick twist in her stomach. Was it fear? She hated how helpless it made her feel. But she'd finally met her match. A creature that could play her at her own game. And that creature was a seagull. If you'd told her that before, she'd have laughed in your face.

She should have run for the tunnels. But now it was too late. Red Eye was putting pictures in her head again. The same pictures as before, only this time, more vivid and powerful and irresistible.

She was in that high place with the four stone dragons. She could see her own scaly pink claws, feel lice scuttling in her feathers.

Her predator's eyes picked up every movement, tiny changes in light and shadow. There! She saw a glitter far below. Was it fish? She spread her wings wide, was about to launch herself on the wind.

"No!" She felt arms dragging her back. Her eyes snapped open. She froze with terror. Below her was the cliff edge. Then nothing, just a dizzying drop into the bay.

It was Ellis who'd grabbed her. He pulled her further back.

"What are you doing!" he shouted at her. "You were walking off the edge of the cliff!"

"I thought I could fly," said Meriel.

"Are you crazy?" Ellis yelled at her.

"I was in this place somewhere," she said. "High up, with stone dragons."

Ellis stared at her. "Stone dragons?" He was used to Meriel being vague and mystical. But this time, she made no sense at all. "I don't understand. What are you talking about?"

He couldn't hide his shock and alarm. Had she really been going to step off that cliff? Into thin air? She'd had her arms outspread, her eyes closed. She'd looked really happy! "What are you talking about?" demanded Ellis again.

But instead of answering, Meriel gazed into the sky. Above the fog layer, up in the sunshine, two big gull shapes were circling lazily. Red Eye and the gull with the black leg band.

"Gulls!" said Ellis, alarmed. "Come on!" He covered his head and scuttled in a crouching run for the tunnel entrance.

But they didn't attack. It was as if, Meriel thought, Red Eye didn't mean to kill her. Not this time. He was just teasing her, like a cat with a mouse. To amuse himself maybe, to test his power.

If she could get inside his mind she'd know for sure.

But he wouldn't let her in; he was wise to her tricks. And besides, she was scared. Red Eye's mind was probably a nightmare place to be.

Back down in the tunnels, Meriel seemed to Ellis to be back to normal. She was talking sense again. "We've got to move from here," she said. "Red Eye knows where we're hiding. And there was another gull with him, with a black leg band."

"That's Jet!" said Danny. "He's my tame gull. I saved his life. I raised him from a chick."

"You never told us about him," said Ellis, accusingly. "Why didn't you tell us?"

"Anyway, he's not your tame gull any more," added Meriel. "He looked really friendly with Red Eye just now."

"And I was going to tell you, Danny!" TJ burst out, leaping up and pacing around the den. "That's how I got caught! I poked my head out of the tunnel, looking for you coming back. And this gull was there! I nearly wet myself! Then I thought, *It's only Jet!* 'Cos he had this black leg band. And then he flew off. So I climbed out. But he came back, Danny. And he was leading the others. Right to me!"

"In other words," said Meriel, "he betrayed your friend TJ. So don't trust him. He'll betray you."

Danny bit his lip and looked stubborn. "He wouldn't betray me," he muttered.

"*Huh!*" snorted Meriel. "I bet he hates all humans now. Just like Red Eye does. Red Eye only lets them live if they're useful to him, like the Creepers are or the food collectors."

The thought flashed through her mind: *Well, why is he letting me live then?* It was as if Red Eye had some use for her, some purpose in mind.

"Jet doesn't hate me," insisted Danny. "I saved his life, he used to follow me around like a pet dog!"

He left out the bit about driving Jet away, shouting at him and chucking stones. Because, deep in his heart, he'd told himself, *Jet understands. He knows I did it for his own good.*

After all, hadn't Mum said, "*That bird's almost human*"?

Ellis butted in, "Look, I don't know about this Jet. But I know we've got to get out of these tunnels."

"Why?" said Danny. "Just because *she* says so?" He shot a hostile look at Meriel.

"If she says so, you'd better listen," said Ellis.

Information Meriel had given him, about what animals would do, had saved his life more than once.

"The gulls won't come down here," said TJ.

"No, but they'll stand guard outside," said Meriel, "so we can't get out. We could starve down here."

"We've got to move," said Ellis, urgently. "Now, while it's still foggy." His old horror had come back. It freaked him out, thinking of being trapped down here, in these tunnels.

"Where, though?" asked TJ. "Where can we go where the gulls and the Creepers won't look?"

"Wonderland," said Danny, suddenly.

"But that's their neighbourhood," said TJ. "That's where they nest, raise their chicks!"

Meriel looked with new respect at Danny. "It's a good idea," she said. "Right where the gulls live. It's the last place they'll look."

From the high tower of the Town Hall, Red Eye gazed down. Up here he was in bright sunlight.

But Mackenzie Point, far below, was strangely hushed and peaceful. Most of it was still hidden under swirling fog. The fog was clearing though. Soon the gulls in Wonderland would start flying again, squabbling and fighting as usual, scattering white feathers like snow.

Then Red Eye's bodyguard would go out on patrol. Two of them, Pirate and Zapper, sat on a ledge below him. They were having a tug of war with a sand eel.

"*Hwak, hwak!*" croaked Pirate, snatching the eel and stabbing Zapper in the eye.

Red Eye was still in control. But he knew he had to keep a tight hold on his rowdy mob of gulls, show them who was boss. The Creepers too, and the food-collecting slaves, needed reminding.

"*Kawrrr!*" shrieked Red Eye, strutting along the ledge, his ruby eyes glinting.

He was preparing a little demonstration. Everyone, gulls and humans, would be here in the Town Square, to watch. The demonstration would do two things. It would show his power. And it would get rid of this new human. The one his best spy, Jet, had led him to. Two intruders had somehow slipped past the sentries into Mackenzie Point. The boy didn't interest Red Eye – the skuas could deal with him. But the girl surprised him.

She had a very unhuman-like mind. It almost rivalled his own. Almost, but not quite. He was stronger. He'd proved that, just now, on the cliffs, when he'd made her do his bidding. It wasn't the boy who'd saved her. Red Eye could have made her jump, if he'd wanted to. But he didn't want to – it wasn't the right place, or time.

"*Kwarr!*" He screamed his war cry again, even louder.

Down on the ledge below, Zapper and Pirate stopped squabbling. They hunched, heads down, making meek *mewing* sounds.

If any gull displeased him, Red Eye's punishment was swift and terrible. It wasn't only puffins he turned inside out with a few shakes of his beak.

Red Eye hopped onto the head of a stone dragon. There were four of them, one on each corner of the tower, facing north, south, east and west.

He clacked his cruel hooked beak. Then spread out his great wings so that they glittered like silver in the sunshine.

His demonstration would take place before the day was out.

Chapter Nine

"Don't carry too much," said Ellis, as TJ and Danny collected up sleeping bags and the other stuff they'd got from their night-time raids on empty houses.

"And you should take off that armour," he told Danny. "It'll slow you down. And it'll clank, give us away."

"Look," said Danny, "will you stop bossing us about?"

"No, he's right," said TJ. He wouldn't hear a word said against Ellis. Ellis had saved his life. Already, there was hero worship shining in his eyes. "Anyway, you won't need your armour in fog. The gulls won't see you."

Meriel shot Ellis a sharp warning look. It meant, *Just stay cool.* She knew that his fear made him snap out orders. That he hated being trapped in small dark places. That he wanted to get out of here fast before the gulls came and they couldn't get out at all.

Danny muttered, "Oh all right," as he unstrapped the hubcaps. "I'm still keeping my helmet on though," he said.

He wasn't taking any chances. These whizz-kids from the city weren't as useless as he'd thought. They'd saved TJ's life. But he still didn't think they understood how savage the gulls were. Gulls showed no mercy. If they looked down and spied a human head without a red eye somewhere it shouldn't be, they'd dive down and rip at it. He and TJ had talked about shaving their heads. Drawing on their own red eyes, so they could walk safely about the town. But pretending to be Creepers wouldn't work. Soon as they saw you, the real Creepers would alert the gulls. So either way, you got punished.

"They always attack from behind," said Danny. "They come swooping down screaming, rake the back of your head. They've got this call when they attack, this screeching, like, '*Keew! Keew! Keew!*' When you hear that, you'd better run!"

Ellis made himself listen patiently. He knew it was useful information. It was Meriel who said, "We're wasting time."

They slipped out of the tunnels. In the end, TJ and Danny left most of their stuff behind, so they could run faster. Ellis left his backpack too. Except TJ insisted on taking his baseball bat.

"It's still foggy," whispered Ellis. "Good."

"Which way?" said Meriel.

"This way," said Danny. He checked to see if he'd got the key to Wonderland in his pocket. "Okay, let's go."

He was taking them the long way round, through the dunes. He knew the path well, even in fog. He could have taken them by a much shorter route, through the town. But that was far too dangerous.

What if the fog cleared? Apart from the other gulls, and the Creepers, Red Eye was looking down from his high tower. And Red Eye seemed to see everything.

"Keep low," said Danny.

What was left of the fog was down at ground level. It was barely enough to give them cover. Above it, they could see the pale yellow sun.

Ellis thought, *We've left it too late*. He blamed himself. He was the one who insisted, "We've got to go, NOW." They'd have been better off waiting until dark.

He'd seen something. He dropped down on one knee to look closer. A sandy patch was a mass of footprints. They were blurred, hard to see. But he could identify four sets. He knew his own and Meriel's instantly. And those with the stars were TJ's. And he already had Danny's filed away in his mind. When Ellis met anyone for the first time, he always checked out their shoes. In case he had to track them down later.

But there was another set – a stranger's. Big feet, size twelve. Not trainers but wellington boots. Someone heavy who weighed about eighty kilos.

Who hadn't been walking, or running. But just standing here, shifting clumsily from one foot to the other, as if they couldn't decide what to do.

Ellis had seen those prints before, out in the bay. Whoever was out there had been here too, only minutes ago.

"Ellis!" That was Meriel's low voice, calling him through the fog.

With a start, Ellis sprang up. He could lose himself in tracking, just like Meriel did inside an animal's mind. But this wasn't the time to do it. The others had already been swallowed up by the fog. But he tracked them easily, by their footprints, the grass they'd trampled, the tiny striped snail shells they'd crushed. He soon caught up.

Somewhere above them the sun was burning. Now it was as hot in the fog as inside a green house. They had sparkly dewdrops all over them, on their clothes, even their eyelashes. It was like looking through rainbows. Ellis blinked them away.

And another odd thing, they all had their own shadows now, flapping beside them like trapped birds.

"How far is it?" hissed Ellis. The fog was

thinning. Soon it would disappear and they'd have no cover.

But they were already here, stepping over a collapsed wire fence, going in the back way. Ellis was treading on something. It was an old broken sign. He could just make out the faded letters: *Wonderland*.

They crept between the iron legs of the roller coaster. Above them, in a forest of girders, gulls were roosting. A single white feather came drifting down.

TJ glanced up, terrified. His chest felt tight; he could barely breathe. He couldn't see them, but he could hear them, hundreds of them, right over his head. It was Gull City up there. He could hear the scratchy rustling of their feathers. Their beaks clicking.

The acrid stink of their droppings was so strong it made your eyes water.

"Keew!" one screeched through the mist. TJ nearly jumped out of his skin. He gripped his baseball bat tighter, as he crept on. His knuckles showed white as bone.

"Splat!" A white oily dropping splashed over his shoe.

Then it happened, what they'd all been fearing. The fog lifted, as if some giant hoover had suddenly sucked it up. They stood, dazzled by the glare, the bright blue sky above. Then they realized the gulls could see them.

"Run!" screamed Danny. He took off, towards an ugly low building, made of breeze blocks. At the same moment, the first gulls came swooping down. TJ lashed out with his baseball bat, whirling it frantically around his head.

Danny fumbled for the Wonderland key. Dropped it, swore, went diving after it.

A screeching gull attacked Ellis. It came from behind just like Danny had said, knocked him flat. Ellis sprawled on the floor, struggled groggily to his knees.

Danny cried out, "The key won't turn!" The lock was rusty. Granddad had said he'd get that fixed! But it didn't help that Danny's fingers were trembling.

"*Keew! Keew!*" The gull darted down for its second run. TJ swished his baseball bat through the air. It caught the gull, a second before its claws ripped open Ellis's neck. The gull bounced off the warehouse wall and, still screeching, fluttered off somewhere.

"They're all coming!" The air above them boiled with wings.

But Danny had got the door open. They dived inside, slammed it shut. Just in time. The gulls thudded against the door, raking it with their beaks and claws.

For a few moments none of them could speak. They crouched on the floor, gasping for breath. Then Danny raised his head.

"Well, that didn't exactly go according to plan," he said, with an accusing glance at Ellis. They were supposed to be sneaking in here under cover of fog. But now the whole gull nation had seen them. Another gull hurled itself against the door.

They were under siege in Wonderland.

Ellis raised his head too. He didn't seem to hear what Danny had just said. Instead, he was staring round.

"Where's Meriel?" he said. "She was just behind me."

Meriel had been making a dash for the Wonderland door, with the gulls squawking and diving around her. Suddenly she'd stopped in her tracks. Red Eye had invaded her mind. She felt herself lifted on feathery wings...

"No!" screamed Meriel, screwing her fists into tight balls, lashing out, as if she could physically fight him off. But there was nothing to hit, only empty air. She stared around amazed. The other gulls had stopped their attack. They had retreated, and were sitting in rows on the roller coaster. Why? She was at their mercy, an easy target.

Then Meriel saw why. A lone gull, pure white, majestic, sat on top of the helter-skelter. His lizard neck craned this way and that as he surveyed his subjects. It was Red Eye.

"Kew! Kew! Kew!"

One reckless young gull dived, shrieking, for Meriel's head. Zapper snatched him out of the sky, threw him squawking away like a piece of litter. The other gulls bowed and *mewed* submissively. They'd got the message. Even though she wasn't a Creeper, this human was to be left alone. She was under Red Eye's protection.

Now the rows of gulls had even stopped mewing. They were silent, as if waiting for something.

Red Eye waited, as if testing their obedience. Not one of them moved. Proud and triumphant, he beat his great white wings. *"Kwarrr!"* That cry meant, "I am invincible!"

As his scream shattered the silence. Meriel trembled. She looked up. That was a mistake. The great gull's ruby eyes locked with hers. She felt her will power crumbling to dust.

And then, she had no fears at all. She knew, with absolute confidence, where she was heading. She was going to that high tower, where there were stone dragons. She could see it in her mind. She could see herself too, flying from its top, soaring over Mackenzie Point. There were her slaves below her scuttling about like ants! The Creepers' red eyes, staring up.

She wasn't Meriel any more. She was a massive gull, with pure snowy white feathers and ruby eyes and a cruel, hooked yellow beak.

A Creeper was watching, hiding in the dunes, just outside the wire fence of Wonderland. He was seventeen, tall and big and clumsy. He had wellington boots on his size twelve feet. He didn't have a clue what was going on.

He saw a girl with wild, tangled hair. She came striding out of Wonderland, head held high. Above her Red Eye was lazily flapping, as if leading the way. They were going towards the Town Square. Then there was a great rustling and squawking above him, a fluttering of wings. The other gulls took off, streaming through the sky after Red Eye's bodyguard. They were going to the Town Square too.

The Creeper crouched there, until the gulls had all gone and the sky was empty. Then he came out from his hiding place. His face was twisted in anguish. He gazed after the gulls. Then at the closed door in the low breeze-block building. He clawed at the red eye on top of his shaved head, as if he wanted to rip it off. But it wouldn't come off. It was marked in indelible pen. So then he just stood there, shuffling his big boots in the sand, trying to decide what to do next.

CHAPTER TEN

Inside the breeze-block building, Ellis and TJ crouched among the ancient arcade machines.

"Where is she?" said Ellis. "I'm sure she was right behind me."

"Maybe the gulls got her," said TJ.

"Shut up!" said Ellis.

Danny had dashed off to get candles. "Granddad keeps some in the storeroom," he'd said.

Even in the dark, he seemed to know this place like the back of his hand. Suddenly candles flared.

"*Aaargh!*" TJ staggered back. A chalk-white face with thick red lips and frizzy orange hair sprang out of the shadows.

"It's only the dancing clown," said Danny. "It's one of the machines."

He'd always hated that clown. It was so spooky. If you put a penny in the slot it sprang to life. Its legs and arms jerked grotesquely about. And it had a horrible loud mocking laugh – "*HA HA HA HA HA!*" – that you could hear even outside the building.

There was a knock at the door.

"Meriel!" said Ellis. "I knew those gulls didn't get her!"

He ran to open it.

"Careful!" said Danny. "Careful no gulls get in."

So Ellis opened the door a crack. "Creeper!" he warned the others. He tried to slam the door shut. But the Creeper, much stronger and bigger than him, barged it open and came stomping in. TJ shrank back among the arcade machines.

Danny sprang up, yelling. "What'd you let him in for? That's Cal, TJ's brother!"

Danny turned his red, furious face to Cal. "What you doing here? What you doing? Spying for the gulls? Trying to trap us? You stood there! Just *stood there*! While they tried to kill your own brother!"

Words failed him. He rushed at Cal, swinging wildly. He kicked him, punched him with his fists. Cal didn't even try to fight back. He just took the blows, as if he deserved them.

Danny backed off, panting. Cal wiped blood off his nose. "I did try to find him!" he burst out. "I got lost in the fog. And I wanted to join you, Danny! To fight the gulls!"

"Then why didn't you?" Danny spat out.

Cal struggled to find the words. He was big, clumsy and dumb-looking. Before he became a Creeper, people used to make fun of him – his own father the most. But his dad had disappeared. Then Cal had become a Creeper. For the first time in his life he got respect from people. But it all fell apart again when he saw what they did to TJ.

"I hung around outside the tunnels," he said. "I couldn't get down the hole. I was gonna call out but..."

He couldn't explain why he hadn't. Grief for TJ,

shame at not acting earlier, horror at what the gulls had done. But also fear, that Danny, TJ's best friend, would drive him away in disgust. All these emotions had been mixed up in his mind.

And Danny was raging at him, saying all the things he feared. "You scumbag Creeper! Think we're going to trust you? Pretending you tried to save TJ? You didn't even like him!"

Again, Cal wrung his massive hands. It was true, he'd been mean to TJ sometimes. But he'd been jealous of him. Cal wasn't very good with words but again he struggled to explain. "Dad said TJ was his favourite. Dad said, 'At least he's got brains. You're just a useless lump!'"

Something moved amongst the machines. TJ came out. He was staring at Cal. And when he spoke, it was to Cal alone, as if no one else was there. "But he always told me you were his favourite! He said I was too soft. He said, 'You big girl! Why can't you be tough like your brother?'"

Cal ignored all that. His mouth hung open. He rubbed his eyes as if they were playing tricks on him. "You're alive!"

"Yeah," Danny butted in. "Ellis rescued him.

That guy that just opened the door for you. *He* rescued him! Went out into the bay! He didn't just stand there, watching."

"I didn't!" protested Cal, still staring at TJ as if he was seeing a ghost.

TJ was staring back. He'd had a big shock too. He'd just learned that their dad had bullied them both. That he'd deliberately turned them against each other. TJ had had no idea, none at all, that Cal was suffering too.

How could he know so little about his own brother?

But Danny was yelling in TJ's face, "Don't trust him. He's just lying, about coming to save you."

Cal had given up speaking. He just stood there, still gazing at TJ. One big hand, automatically, went to his shaven head and started rubbing at that red eye. He looked like a cross between a big fierce ogre and a little kid in distress.

Then Ellis stepped in. "He's not lying," he said.

Danny swung round, angrily. "What do you know about it?"

"I saw his footprints. Out in the bay. And by the tunnels. He's telling the truth."

"Yeah, and so what?" said Danny. "I still think Red Eye sent him here. To try to get us to go outside. So the gulls can kill us."

"There's no gulls outside," said Cal. "They've all gone towards the Town Square. After the girl."

"What girl?" said Ellis, urgently. "Do you mean Meriel?"

Cal stared at him, bewildered. He didn't know any Meriel. He didn't even know where Ellis had come from. He was still trying to cope with finding TJ alive, when he thought he'd been drowned on the mudflats.

"What was she like, this girl? Little, with like long, black hair?" demanded Ellis. "Did the gulls hurt her?"

"No." Slowly, Cal shook his big, shaved head. "That was the weird thing. They never touched her. They just followed her and Red Eye. It was like he was taking her someplace."

Someplace? thought Ellis, his mind racing. Didn't Meriel say something weird about a high place? He struggled to remember. A high place, *with stone dragons*?

"Are there any stone dragons around here?" he

asked Danny, since TJ and Cal seemed too stunned to answer. They were still staring, as if they'd never seen each other before.

"Stone dragons?" said Danny. "What's that got to do with anything?"

Cal suddenly slapped himself on the head – *Whack!* – as if he was trying to clear it. "There's stone dragons at the top of the Town Hall tower," he said. "Really high up. Red Eye sits on them."

Ellis felt a chill around his heart. "I hope she's not going up there." Terrible suspicions clawed at his mind.

"Why should she?" asked Danny.

"She thinks she can fly," said Ellis.

"What?" said Danny. But Ellis was already running for the door.

"Don't go out there!" said Danny. "That's just what Cal wants. He's a Creeper, remember!"

But Ellis had already burst out of the door. He was haring for the nearest cover, in a crouching run, his arms folded over his head when, suddenly, he stopped…

Slowly, very slowly, he took his arms off his head, stared upwards. At first the sun dazzled him.

He shaded his eyes. The great guano wedding cakes of the Big Wheel and roller coaster were completely empty. So was the sky. There were no squawking gull mobs. They had gone – only their stink remained. And it was so silent, you could hear the sea, its waves *swooshing* round the shores of Mackenzie Point.

Ellis took a big, deep breath. Danny and TJ stumbled out of the building, stared round in wonder.

Cal said, "See? I told you."

"My brother was telling the truth," said TJ.

"Huh!" said Danny, throwing ugly looks at Cal. "I still don't trust him. We'd be crazy to go to the Town Square. What if it's a trap?"

"Look," said Ellis, "if you don't want to come with me, don't. I don't need your help."

"I'll help you," said TJ. "And so will Cal." He turned to his big brother. Danny had already mentioned about the rescue out on the mudflats. But TJ didn't think Cal had taken it in. He wanted to make extra sure that Cal understood how much they owed to Ellis.

"Ellis saved my life out there in the bay," he explained to Cal. "I'd really lost it – I thought, *I'm gonna* die*!* And he just came out of the fog. Like some kind of miracle!"

Ellis shook his head, impatiently. "It wasn't a miracle," he muttered. "I was just tracking. Anyway," he added, "it wasn't just me. You were great out there in the bay. You didn't panic. You were brave."

"Was I?" said TJ. That wasn't how he remembered it. But, if Ellis said so, it must be true. *Hey, I'm brave,* TJ thought, as if he'd made a new, amazing discovery about himself.

Ellis was already hurrying away, towards the Town Square.

TJ and Cal ran after him. And, after a moment's hesitation, Danny followed.

Chapter Eleven

Red Eye sat at the top of his high tower. He preened himself in the mirror medallions of the dead Mayor's chain. A cruel yellow beak and glittering eye stared back at him.

"*Kwarr!*" he shrieked, beating his huge wings.

He fluttered onto the head of the west-facing stone dragon, his favourite perch.

"*Kwarr!*" he screamed again.

The grey wrinkled ocean stretched to the far horizon. He felt that he owned the world.

He felt invincible, godlike. He had the power of life and death. Soon, he would send the human plunging down into the Town Square. By the strength of his mind alone. It would be a lesson for all his subjects. But it was also Red Eye showing off. Saying, "See what I can do! Look at my powers and tremble!"

The scene was set. His gull subjects were here. So were the Creepers. Some of the slaves had been marched from the school. You didn't need to bring the whole lot. The few who saw would tell the others. Then they would fear their gull masters even more. And Red Eye most of all. Even though they hardly ever saw him close up. For them, he was just a distant white glow at the top of a high tower.

The only thing missing was Meriel. But she would be here very soon. Red Eye had seen her crossing the square and going into the Town Hall. She'd stepped confidently, her head held high, her neck turning this way and that.

No one touched her. The Creepers shrank back. Even Zapper and Snapper stopped their racket. It was clear by now that this human belonged to Red Eye. That he had chosen her for some purpose of his own.

Inside the building, Meriel crossed the banqueting hall. It had once been splendid, with long stained-glass windows and portraits of all the past mayors of Mackenzie Point hanging on the walls. They stared down, looking solemn and important.

But the place was a wreck now. Red Eye's skua bodyguard had taken it over – smashed through the windows and splashed their smelly white droppings everywhere.

Pirate was gobbling a starfish on the banqueting table.

"*Ack! Ack! Ack!*" He gave an ear-splitting screech as Meriel passed. He knew he mustn't attack her, he was just acting tough.

But Meriel turned. One glance from her eyes was enough.

"*Mew, mew!*" Pirate cringed down low, until his beak touched the table, something he only usually did with Red Eye himself.

Meriel began climbing the narrow twisty stairs that led to the top of the high tower.

Down below, Ellis, TJ, Danny and Cal were hiding behind the butcher's shop. It had shut down years ago, long before the gulls came. Boarded-up, derelict shops surrounded the Town Square. Weeds pushed up through its cobbles.

Ellis thought, *Am I dreaming?*

Here he was, in this crumbling little seaside town. He was peering out into the Town Square. A weird audience was assembled. Gulls crowded on every rotting roof and window-sill. Their silence seemed more sinister than their screams. The Creepers stood in silence too. Ellis's skin crawled. Were they watching with their human eyes? Or that big red eye on their shaved skulls?

The slaves hardly dared look up. They were a wretched bunch, with matted hair and ragged clothes. Some had bare feet. But everyone – gulls, Creepers, slaves – seemed to be waiting for something.

Ellis thought again, *This isn't real.*

Then, looking up like all the rest at the high tower, he saw a face at a window. A window near the top, with all the glass smashed out.

Meriel? he thought.

Of course it was. And those suspicions he'd had leaped back into his brain like roaring monsters.

He's going to make her jump!

Just like he almost had on the cliff. That must have been a trial run. Ellis understood it all now. Why, ever since they'd arrived at Mackenzie Point, Meriel had been even more distant than usual.

She hadn't wanted to admit it − her pride wouldn't let her. But, from the beginning, Red Eye must have been playing tricks with her mind.

"I'm going up there," said Ellis, pointing to the tower. "You stay here."

Ellis began sneaking round the back of the shops. With any luck, he could reach the Town Hall without being seen. TJ, Cal and Danny looked at each other helplessly. What should they do now?

Then Danny, gazing again at the Town Hall, saw a gull he recognized winging its way towards the tower. "Jet," he whispered. You couldn't mistake that leg band. And anyway, he could always pick out Jet, even without the band, from a hundred other gulls.

Jet came flying in from the west, landed for a brief moment on the dragon next to Red Eye. They touched beaks in greeting. Then Jet fluttered down to a lower ledge. He too was waiting to watch the show.

"Jet," muttered Danny, miserably.

So it was true, what TJ and Meriel had said, that Jet was firmly on the side of the gulls. That he was Red Eye's right-hand man.

What else did you expect? thought Danny, after the way he'd shouted at Jet, driven him away.

But still, in his heart, there'd been a tiny flickering hope. *Jet wouldn't betray me.*

He remembered when he'd first found Jet, a pitiful bundle of fluff. How, when he'd picked him up, his body had been feather light. But it had been warm and Danny had felt Jet's tiny heart beating against his fingers.

Without knowing it, Danny, trying to get a better look at Jet, had moved out into the square.

"Danny," hissed TJ. "What are you doing?"

He was going to run out, drag him back. But it was too late. The Creepers had seen him. Two came pounding over. Danny recognized them. One had been their next-door neighbour. But it was no use saying, "Hi, Mr. Robinson! Remember me?" He wasn't Mr. Robinson any more. He was a Creeper.

His hatred showed in his eyes.

"We've been looking for you!" he snarled. Danny felt himself gripped by strong arms, frogmarched towards the other Creepers. "Here's the troublemaker! One of those Dillons."

The Creepers closed around him. Hidden behind the butcher's shop, Cal and TJ knew they couldn't save Danny. As soon as they showed themselves, the Creepers and gulls would attack. They already had TJ on their hit list. And, by now, they'd know Cal was a traitor too.

"I know!" said Cal. "We'll go to the school, set the other slaves free!"

"Think they'll help us?" said TJ. He thought of the shuffling zombie-like slaves collecting shellfish and crabs. They seemed barely alive – crushed by exhaustion, starvation and fear.

Cal shook his head. "I don't know if they'll help." But what else was there to do?

"Better take the long way round," said TJ. "Through the dunes."

And, together, the two brothers hurried towards the school...

* * *

Danny had Creepers all around him. Their faces were ugly. Their shaved heads sweated. He could feel their hot breath.

"Dillons must all be wiped out," said one, who was a retired policeman. "They plot against the gulls. They break the law!"

The circle of Creepers moved closer. They looked like they wanted to tear him to bits. One was Miss Sillitoe. She'd been the town librarian, before it too had closed.

"Jet!" shrieked Danny desperately. "Jet, help me!"

Up on his high tower, Red Eye saw a commotion below. The Creepers had caught a human. An enemy of the gulls, who needed punishing. He didn't take much notice. He could leave it to them; they liked punishing lawbreakers. It seemed they didn't even need the gulls to help. He saw a ring of big red eyes, moving in on their victim.

Then he heard a fluttering below him. He saw Jet take off, glide over the square on strong wings. Again, he didn't take much notice. He just assumed Jet was taking charge. Jet had been very useful to him. He, of all the gulls, seemed to understand Red

Eye's human subjects – their pathetic fears and weaknesses.

"*Kiaow!*" Red Eye croaked in satisfaction. His eyes glittered. His great clawed feet stamped on the dragon's head.

Meriel came crawling out onto the ledge that ran round all four sides of his tower. The wind was whipping her long hair. The ledge had no railings. But she looked entirely unafraid.

Red Eye didn't feel pity. It was natural for him to kill his rivals. Not that humans were much of a challenge. But of all the humans he'd met, this one interested him the most.

"*Kiaow!*" said Red Eye again, almost as if he was welcoming her to his world in the sky.

Suddenly, screams and shouts came from the square below. Red Eye's snake neck whipped round. He gazed down. What was going on down there? At first he couldn't believe it.

Then "*Ack! Ack! Ack!*" he screeched in fury.

Jet was attacking the Creepers! Pecking their necks, driving them away. Instead of punishing the prisoner, he was protecting him.

Red Eye didn't hesitate. Didn't even pause to be

surprised that his best spy had turned traitor. This was serious insubordination. It must be dealt with immediately.

With a blood-chilling shriek of pure rage, Red Eye came hurtling down from his high tower.

CHAPTER TWELVE

Ellis was lucky. He'd reached the Town Hall without being attacked. There was some kind of trouble in the square behind him. But he didn't dare stop to look. He raced up the wide, white-streaked steps. Then slipped inside the big wooden doors.

He thought, *How do I get up to the tower?*

Then he didn't need to wonder. He crouched down. There were Meriel's tracks in the gull guano. All he had to do was follow.

His luck held. The banqueting hall seemed empty. The gulls must be all outside in the Town Square. He looked around.

They've really trashed this place, he thought.

It stank to high heaven. The floor, walls and furniture were slimy with a mixture of droppings, fish bones and guts. A breeze gusted in through the shattered windows. Only a few shards of glass, ruby, green and blue, were still left in them, like wobbly teeth.

Grimacing, Ellis picked his way through the mess. He was concentrating hard on tracking Meriel. He saw another of her footprints beside a small open door.

The way to the tower, thought Ellis. He hurried towards it.

Then he stopped dead. His sharp ears had picked up a sound. The hairs rose on the back of his neck.

It was the scratchy rustling of a gull's feathers.

He whirled round. Pirate was watching him from the banqueting table. A starfish leg was dangling from his beak. His beady eyes glittered.

For a second, Ellis stood frozen. Then *"Ack! Ack!*

Ack!" Pirate screamed for back-up. There was a blur of white wings, an explosion of ruby glass, as Zapper burst through the window.

But Ellis was already under the banqueting table. It was a long table that stretched down the room. He galloped beneath it on all fours. He saw beaks, eyes, as the two gulls swooped and snapped.

Ellis had reached the end of the table. Now there was no cover. He dashed for the door.

"Ow!" yelled Ellis as Pirate raked his neck. But then he was through. He slammed the door behind him, trapping Pirate's wing. Pirate screeched, wrenched his wing free, leaving feathers behind. On the other side of the door, Ellis collapsed, gasping. That was close.

But he was safe, for the moment.

He felt the gash on the back of his neck, cleaned it with spit. It stung like crazy. Taking a deep breath, he started climbing the twisty stairs to the tower.

Outside in the Town Square, Danny stared upwards. He could still hardly believe it – that Jet had swooped down to his rescue.

He doesn't hate me after all, thought Danny, shaking his head in wonder. *He remembers when we were friends.*

But now Jet was paying the price for switching sides. Above Danny, he was fighting for his life.

When Red Eye had come hurtling down like a thunderbolt, the Creepers had backed off. Now Danny stood alone, in the centre of the square. He was the only one staring upwards. All the others – gulls, Creepers and slaves – were still as statues. They had their heads bowed in the presence of Red Eye, their eyes cast down.

"You can do it, Jet!" shrieked Danny, even though he knew Jet couldn't hear him. "You can beat him!"

Danny punched the air in frustration. He was desperate to help Jet. But there was nothing he could do. Jet was on his own up there, against a super gull.

The two great gulls had clashed, right above the square. Gone for each other with beaks and claws. There'd been feathers flying everywhere.

But where was Red Eye now? Only Jet hovered above Danny. For a few seconds the sky seemed empty. Had Jet won? Had Red Eye given up?

No chance. He had only just started.

Red Eye came screaming in from the north like an avenging angel. He had a stone in his claws, picked up from the shore. He dropped it right over Jet's head, screeching in triumph.

The stone bounced off Jet's skull. Stunned, he went spiralling down, landing on the flat roof of the library. Red Eye was right behind him.

"*Ka, ka, ka!*" screeched Red Eye, diving in for the kill.

The air was full of noise and whirling feathers. While down below, in the square, there was only spooky silence and a sea of bowed heads.

Red Eye spread his wings over the fallen Jet, then grabbed him by his neck and twisted. Like a wrestler, he forced Jet onto his back. Jet was helpless. Now Red Eye was dragging him along the roof, shaking him like a rag doll.

"Oh, Jet," whispered Danny. He stuffed his fist into his mouth, to stop himself from sobbing. It seemed that Jet was done for.

Why had he ever thought Jet could win? Red Eye was bigger, stronger and much, much smarter.

Danny looked round desperately for something to throw. Crouching down, he tried to prise up a cobble stone using his fingernails.

"Ouch!" He'd almost ripped a nail off. But the stone didn't shift. He tried another. This one came loose. Would the Creepers stop him? Danny didn't care. With bloody fingers, he hurled his pathetic missile. He didn't aim high enough. It clattered harmlessly off the library's boarded-up windows. Danny cursed.

But the noise took Red Eye's attention. Only for a second, but long enough for Jet to wriggle from beneath Red Eye, flip over onto his feet.

Crash! The two great gulls leaped at each other, feathers flying. In the silent square you could hear their wing blows.

Red Eye took off, made a wild, wide sweep over Mackenzie Point. Jet soared after him. The epic aerial battle was on again.

CHAPTER THIRTEEN

At the top of the tower, Ellis wasn't aware of the fight between Jet and Red Eye that was raging over Mackenzie Point. It seemed as if he and Meriel were in their own little world up here.

Ellis had taken one glance at the dizzying drop, felt sick and didn't look again. Now his whole concentration was on Meriel.

He'd squeezed through a tiny window, crawled

along the ledge. All his limbs were trembling. One wrong move and he'd go plunging down into the square below.

He could see Meriel now. "Don't move!" he begged her. But she didn't seem scared of falling. Somehow, she'd climbed onto Red Eye's favourite perch – the dragon on the west corner. She crouched on it, frog-like, her long hair streaming out behind her.

Meriel stared down over Mackenzie Point, surveying her kingdom. Her neck twisted this way and that, with jerky, gull-like movements. She felt godlike, invincible. She had the power of life and death. Even over humans.

"Meriel," begged Ellis again, creeping closer. "Come back down with me." He was near now – he could almost reach out and touch her.

Meriel turned to him slowly. Who was this human, who'd dared to climb her high tower?

She threw back her head. Her mouth gaped open like a crimson cave. Out of it came a savage, inhuman cry: *"Kwarrr!"*

One hand gripped the dragon's neck. With the other, she swiped at Ellis, trying to rake out his eyes. She was making more creepy gull noises, deep in her throat: *"Kak, kak, kak!"*

She lashed out again, fingers clawed like talons. Ellis shrank back. "Quit that. Now! It's me, Ellis!"

Watch it! he warned himself. He'd almost overbalanced; his shoe had skidded on something. He hugged the tower wall, shivering, the wind tugging his clothes. He dared to look down. He saw a heavy chain at his feet, with glinting medallions. What was something like that doing up here? But Ellis had no time to wonder about it.

"Kawrr!" screamed Meriel again, her eyes flashing fury.

Very carefully, Ellis backed round the corner. He peeped out.

Now she couldn't see him, she seemed to have forgotten his existence. She was still squatting on the stone dragon. She spread out her arms like wings...

"You're human," Ellis pleaded. "Humans can't fly!"

If she heard him, she didn't show it. She lifted her face, let the wind caress it.

"You're Meriel," yelled Ellis, searching frantically in his mind for things to remind her. "Remember that time we first met? After my mum and dad got shot? And you and the Prof came to Africa to get me? And White-Face went ape one day. And I thought, *He's going to tear me apart!* And you said, real cool, 'He's just showing off.' And I thought, *That kid Meriel, she's so weird!*"

Ellis forced out a laugh, "*Ha, ha, ha!*" It didn't sound natural at all. More like he was half crazy. Which is what he felt like. Stuck on top of a high tower with Meriel believing she was Red Eye and could fly like a bird.

Down in the square, Danny wasn't watching the high tower. He had eyes only for Jet. The savage fight between him and Red Eye was still raging, over the rooftops of Mackenzie Point. Then out over the dunes.

"Get him, Jet!" shrieked Danny, desperately.

He'd hoped, until the last moment, that Jet would win. That some miracle might happen. But Red Eye was much too powerful, pecking, beating Jet with his mighty wings, wearing him down. Jet had put up a heroic fight. But he was flagging, sinking lower in the sky. Danny could see blood streaking his feathers. Then Red Eye came screeching in for the last attack: *"Keew, keew, keew!"*

He swivelled in mid-air and, feet-first like a velociraptor, he clawed at Jet's head.

Jet fluttered. But then his wings folded. He was finished. Danny watched in horror as Jet plummeted down into the dunes.

Danny couldn't see where Jet had fallen. But Red Eye could. He was diving down to finish him off. Then he'd swoop back to the tower, where he'd screech in triumph as Meriel went tumbling to earth, reminding all his subjects just who ruled.

But then Red Eye saw Ellis, clinging to the ledge. Jet could wait for a moment. Two humans sent to their deaths was an even better lesson. After that, and the way he'd just clobbered Jet, none of his subjects would even *dream* of defying him.

"Kwarr!"

It had been a good day. In a relaxed way, Red Eye went gliding back to the tower. He was beautiful in flight, breathtaking. His great wings, glinting in the sun, were as snowy white as an angel's.

He didn't anticipate any trouble. Meriel was brainwashed. Poor, pathetic human, she thought she could fly. If Red Eye had any sense of humour, which he didn't, he'd have laughed at that.

The other human he'd just whack off the ledge with one wing blow.

He swooped in, meaning to deal first with Ellis, cowering on the ledge.

But suddenly Ellis sprang up. Something gleamed in his hand. It was the golden chain.

Swaying wildly, Ellis whirled it round his head like a slingshot. He let it go. It went twisting through the air...

Then Ellis felt himself falling. Frantically, he lunged for the north dragon, grabbed its neck. But his feet had slipped off the ledge, were dangling in mid-air.

Red Eye, the gold chain tangled around him, swerved away. From below Danny saw the whole thing. Red Eye was screeching, trying to free himself. It seemed, for a few minutes, that the great super gull could still fly, even tied up in the chain. He was out over the sea now. He seemed indestructible!

The medallions flashed even brighter than the

sun. But then suddenly, unexpectedly, the heavy chain dragged him down. Red Eye went hurtling towards the sea. As he plunged into the grey water, his gold fire went out. The waves closed over him. There were a few ripples. Then the surface of the sea was still.

Danny thought, *It's over*. He could hardly believe it.

But he didn't cheer. He just felt numb and cold. "Jet's dead too," he whispered to himself. Jet had died trying to protect him.

Danny was so mixed up. He'd wanted Jet to remember him, to be on his side, not Red Eye's. But now he thought, *I wish I hadn't shouted for him. Made him choose. It's all my fault.*

High above the Town Square, Meriel was staring round, bewildered.

Red Eye's fall had released her mind. At first she had no idea where she was. Then she saw sky, clouds spinning around her, then a dizzying drop.

With a shocked gasp she realized. "I'm on top of the tower!"

She wobbled and almost fell. She clutched at the dragon's neck. "How'd I get up here?" she thought, horrified. But then a panicky voice screamed close by, "Meriel! Help me!"

Her head whirled round. "Ellis!"

He was along the ledge, his arms hooked over another stone dragon, his feet kicking in space. He was trying to haul himself up but his hands were slipping, his fingernails scrabbling on the slimy gull droppings.

Meriel scooted along the ledge, grabbed the back of Ellis's jacket and hauled with all her strength.

"Stop kicking, I've got you," she said.

It flashed, crazily, through Ellis's mind: *I'm falling! How can she sound so cool?* But then with one desperate lunge, he got a grip again on the stone dragon and heaved himself up, until he was lying across its back.

For a minute, he couldn't move. He felt too weak and shattered. He took deep, shuddering breaths while his mind told him, *It's okay, you're safe, you're safe.*

Finally, he slithered, shakily, along the dragon's crested spine back to the ledge. Meriel was sitting hunched up, against the tower wall, her arms hugging her knees. She couldn't remember much – later she might. But she still had a pretty good idea what had happened.

"Red Eye took over my mind, didn't he?"

Ellis didn't answer. He slumped down beside her and closed his eyes. Cloud and blue sky surrounded them. Things were happening, down there in the Town Square, but that seemed so far away.

At last, Ellis opened his eyes. He felt a bit better now, more in control. He shot a glance at Meriel.

"Don't worry," she said, as if she knew what he was thinking. "I'm not going to jump."

Ellis took a second, suspicious look. She wasn't making any more gull noises or flapping her arms. She seemed human again. As human as someone like Meriel could ever be.

"We'd better get inside, quick," he told her. "In case Red Eye comes back." He scanned the sky. Ellis couldn't see him. But the great gull could come screaming in out of nowhere.

"Let's go," he said, looking nervously round.

In any case, they needed to get off this tower. Back to TJ and Danny and Cal. As far as Ellis knew, they were still waiting for him, behind the butcher's shop.

He was crawling along to the window, wondering if Pirate was still on guard in the banqueting hall, when he heard Meriel say something behind him. He looked back. She hadn't moved. She was still sitting, huddled up against the wall.

He crawled backwards. "We've got to go!"

"I shouldn't have let him do that," she was muttering. "Take over my mind." She was furious with herself. She was so proud, so fiercely independent. But even she hadn't been able to resist Red Eye.

Ellis tugged at her sleeve. "He'll be back, any second." Red Eye wasn't the kind to give up.

"I don't think he'll come back," said Meriel. "Something's happened to him. He's not in my mind. He's not anywhere."

Ellis stared at her.

In his panic, he'd hurled something at Red Eye. That chain he'd found, lying on the ledge. But then he'd slipped and hadn't seen what had happened. He wasn't even sure he'd hit the gull.

"What do you mean, 'he's not anywhere'?" said Ellis.

Instead of answering, Meriel said, "Look."

She was gazing out at the sky. Suddenly, it was full of gulls, a huge trailing flock of them, streaming out to sea. A shadow fell over the tower as they blocked out the sun.

They flew right overhead, squawking to each other. Ellis automatically covered his head. But they didn't dive to attack. They just carried on flying. And behind them, making the biggest din of all, squabbling and yelping like dogs, came the skua gang: Zapper, Snapper, Hook Beak and the rest.

"What's happening?" asked Ellis, shading his eyes and squinting after them.

"I think they're leaving Mackenzie Point," said Meriel.

They were scattering now, heading off in all directions, some for the far horizon, some heading inland. It seemed that Red Eye's tight control over his kingdom was broken.

Now, for the first time in months, the sky over the little seaside town was empty, clear blue.

Meriel shuddered, as if she was shaking off a nightmare.

"Let's get down there," she said. "Something's

definitely happened to Red Eye."

They climbed down the tower stairs and tiptoed through the wrecked banqueting hall. Tatters of red velvet curtains blew in the breeze. Something clattered. Ellis stopped dead, his heart thudding. But it was only a fragment of blue glass, falling out of a window.

"Pirate must have gone with the others," he said. There was his half-eaten starfish, still on the table.

And then they were outside in the square. There were no gulls. Ellis checked the ledges and rooftops. He couldn't see a single one. It was eerily quiet. Slaves and Creepers were gawping upwards, looking lost and confused. They just couldn't believe that their masters had gone. That Red Eye was no longer on his high tower, watching every move.

Some Creepers, more alert than the rest, were already slipping away into the dunes. As if they didn't want to be around, when the slaves did finally grasp what was going on.

Danny came running over. He looked distraught, almost out of his mind.

"Red Eye's dead," he screamed at them. "He's really dead!"

"You sure?" said Meriel. She'd guessed it herself. But it was still hard to believe.

"Yeah, course I'm sure! He drowned in the sea!" Danny waved his arm frantically out over the waves, to show them. "I saw him go down, right there. And Jet fought him," he went rushing on. "Jet was trying to protect me. But Red Eye, Red Eye..." Danny's voice choked in his throat.

It was Meriel who finished his sentence. "Red Eye killed him?" she said.

She sounded so cold, so indifferent. Danny turned on her, appalled. "You don't care, do you?" he yelled at her. "You don't even care that Jet is dead!"

"Tell us *exactly* what happened," said Meriel. "Did you see Jet die? And try to calm down a bit," she added.

"Calm down!" Danny yelled at her, dancing about with anger. "What do you mean, calm down? Haven't you got any feelings at all? You're such a...a...freak!"

As if a switch had been flipped, Meriel's mood changed. Her eyes darkened with rage, her fists clenched. "Don't you dare call me that!" she spat.

She was ready to pounce, like a tiger. *Freak* was the one word that always made her see red.

Ellis took over. He could see this might end in a major punch-up. He put out his hands, palm downwards, in a peacemaking gesture. "Look, can both of you just cool it?"

He turned to Danny. "All Meriel means is, how do you know for sure Jet is dead? Did you see it with your own eyes?"

To a tracker like Ellis, only seeing was believing.

Danny waved out over the dunes. "Red Eye pecked him. He just fell out the sky, just there!" But then hope sparked in his eyes. He seemed to realize, suddenly, what they were asking him. "You mean, he might still be alive?" he said.

"Might be," said Meriel, whose rages disappeared as quickly as they came. "But don't get your hopes up too high."

It was enough for Danny. "We've got to find him!" he said, dashing off.

"Wait!" said Ellis. He didn't want Danny trampling all over the dunes, wiping out any clues that might lead to where Jet had fallen. "Me and Meriel will find him," he told Danny.

"I'm coming too," insisted Danny, his mouth set in a fierce, stubborn line.

"Just leave it to us," said Meriel. "If Jet's still alive, we'll find him." Danny opened his mouth to protest again but then Meriel added, awkwardly. "I promise."

Danny stared at her. And, suddenly, it didn't matter how freaky he thought she was. Because, somehow, he trusted her. He was sure that, if Meriel gave you her promise, she wouldn't break it.

"All right," he agreed, nodding quietly. "You and Ellis go."

"See you later," Ellis said to Danny as he and Meriel vanished into the dunes.

CHaPTeR
FouRTeen

TJ and Cal were circling through the dunes, to the Mackenzie Point school.

Suddenly, Cal blurted out, "I hated being a Creeper. I did, honest."

He didn't admit that at first it had been great. That he'd swaggered about, feeling for the first time in his life like someone important. He'd even thought, *Dad would be proud of me.*

Then Cal said, "Do you think they drowned Dad? Like they tried to drown you?"

TJ said, "I don't know."

Both brothers stopped. They looked round nervously. As if they expected Dad to pop up and sneer, in his loud bullying voice: "Cal, you're thick as a plank! TJ, you're pathetic, just like your mother!"

Mum had run off years ago. Dad didn't allow any contact with her. He ripped up the birthday cards and binned presents she sent to her sons. TJ didn't even know where she lived.

"He's a big bully!" TJ burst out. He checked quickly over his shoulder. "And I hate him! Do you hate him?"

Cal frowned, unhappily, as if that question was too hard for him to answer. He reached out, twisted a blade of razor grass. It sliced his finger open. But he didn't notice.

"Talk about this later, yeah?" said TJ. Like Cal, he couldn't cope with it now. Besides, there was no time. And what if Dad wasn't really dead? What if he came back? Would he and Cal, together, stand up to him? Or would Dad divide them, just like before?

TJ wasn't sure about that.

The two brothers hurried along in silence. Until Cal said, "There's the school. Get down!"

They flattened themselves into the white dune sand.

The Mackenzie Point Infant and Junior School had closed in June. There weren't enough pupils to keep it open. TJ was due to start secondary school anyway – the same school as Danny, on the mainland.

TJ remembered something, as they lay there, watching the building. *I was so scared! About starting Big School.* He gave a rueful smile. They seemed like a little kid's worries now, from a lifetime ago, before the gulls came. Before he'd had to grow up, far too fast.

"There are no Creepers on guard," whispered Cal, surprised.

Where had they all gone? Maybe they were in the Town Square.

"There's no gulls either!" he whispered, even more amazed. There were always gulls at the school, to back up the Creepers, in case the slaves gave any trouble. "What's going on?"

He wasn't sure what was happening, but it was their big chance to free the slaves. Would they rise in rebellion? Help rescue Danny, join the tiny resistance group in the tunnels?

Dream on! part of Cal's brain told him.

He knew it was a desperate act. But somehow, he had to do it, to make up for becoming a Creeper. To prove to TJ, and to himself, that he could do good things, as well as bad.

"Stay here," he told TJ.

"Wait," said TJ. "What are you going to say to them?"

Cal scrunched up his face. He'd been thinking about that. "I'm going to say, 'Citizens of Mackenzie Point! Don't be scared! I'm not a Creeper any more. I'm on your side! Come with me! Join us! Together we can fight the gulls! Together, we can be free!'"

"Wow!" said TJ, impressed. "That's a great speech!"

"Then," said Cal, "when they're all fired up, first thing we'll do is get Danny back."

"Go for it, bro," said TJ.

He watched Cal stumping over the dunes

towards the school – a big, bear-sized boy, rubbing at the red eye on his shaven head.

He's not dumb, thought TJ, surprised. *He's not dumb at all.*

But Dad had said he was for so long that TJ had believed it. And Cal had believed it too.

The door to the school was locked. Cal kicked it in. The slaves were cowering in the school hall. As soon as they saw a Creeper they started shuffling into line. They thought it was time to go out food collecting.

"No," said Cal. "I've come to set you free!"

They lifted their heads. Some had dull, dead eyes. Some had the eyes of hunted wild animals. Cal knew these people. But when he was a Creeper he'd pretended he didn't – that made the job easier. And now, they were so changed that he truly didn't recognize them. They were all like tattered scarecrows, with long, tangled hair and sunken eyes. Most had peck wounds, where the gulls had punished them, tied up with ragged bandages.

Cal's fine, stirring speech vanished from his mind. Instead, a lump of pity came into his throat and almost choked him.

"Sorry," he mumbled. "Sorry." He couldn't think of what else to say. His mind was like a big black hole.

Then he heard a commotion behind him. He whirled round, ready to defend himself.

But it wasn't the other Creepers. Instead TJ came rushing in. Danny was close behind. Cal barely had time to wonder, *How'd he escape?*

Then TJ was leaping into the air, punching it with his fist. *"Yay!"* he shrieked in excitement. "He's dead! Red Eye is dead!"

CHAPTER
FIFTEEN

In the dunes, Ellis said, "Have you found him yet?"

Meriel shook her head. She'd been trying to connect to Jet's mind, perhaps pick up some clues to his location. But, so far, she'd had no luck.

She concentrated again, shut her eyes. It was easier if the animal was there, right in front of her. But this was like casting out a net, seeing what you caught.

"Nothing," she said. "He's not close."

The other explanation was that Jet was already dead.

Ellis kneeled down again on the sand. It was clean and white, like an untrodden snowdrift. There were no animal tracks, not even the slithering track of a lizard or grass snake. The gulls and the food-collecting slaves had picked these dunes clean weeks ago.

"There must be rabbits at least," said Ellis.

But there were no signs of them. And rabbits always left loads of signs – piles of neat droppings, the prints of their springy back feet and grass stems nibbled by their big buck teeth.

"Haven't found any yet," said Meriel. She'd know if she had. She'd been inside twitchy rabbit minds before. She'd shared their world. She'd frozen with fear when a hawk's shadow fell on her; cowered, trembling with her babies in a dark, smelly burrow.

Meriel knew why there were no rabbits left on Mackenzie Point.

"Red Eye's favourite snack was rabbit babies," said Meriel.

"How'd you know that?" said Ellis.

Meriel shot him a look that said, *How'd you* think *I know?*

"Sorry, I forgot," said Ellis.

Meriel knew much more than he did about Red Eye. She'd been inside his mind. She'd even thought she *was* Red Eye for a while, up on the Town Hall tower.

Ellis thought it best to shut up about that. It was a very touchy subject. Meriel was still mad with herself for letting it happen.

"We're not doing very well here," scowled Meriel, staring at the high dunes that rose around them, stretching from the town, to the sea.

They always got results when they worked as a team like this. Ellis looked for animal signs, while Meriel searched for their mental vibes. Together, they could track down most living creatures.

The trouble was, there wasn't much left alive in these dunes. Most animals had either been eaten, or run away.

"I promised Danny," said Meriel.

Ellis knew this was a big deal for Meriel. She didn't promise often, almost never. But when she did, she never went back on her word.

"We'll find him," said Ellis, scanning the sand again. He didn't add alive or dead. But he couldn't help fearing the worst.

Then he saw a sign. It was very faint, just a scrape through the sand.

He kneeled down excitedly. He did his usual trick of pushing his thumb in the ground, to compare his fresh print with the track. It was a quick way of checking how old it was.

"It's just been made," said Ellis. "It could be a wing tip, you know, dragging on the ground." A dragging wing meant an injured bird.

"Think it's Jet?" asked Meriel.

"I think there's a good chance."

Meriel closed her eyes, cancelled out her own, human thoughts. She was searching now, like you tune a radio, trying to pick up the right station.

And suddenly, she was locked on. Pain slammed into her; pain that made her give sharp, wild shrieks. Her sight was blurred – there was darkness, then a circle of light. Then darkness again. Her head flopped forward, her beak dug into the sand. Too weak to resist, she was being sucked away, into deeper darkness...

"Meriel!" Ellis was shaking her. Meriel opened her eyes. She was back in her own body. The pain was gone, and the blackness. The dazzling white dunes were all around and there was Ellis's concerned face, shouting into hers. "Meriel?"

"I found Jet," said Meriel. "I think he's dying."

"Where?" said Ellis.

They could have followed the prints of his dragging wing. But that would have taken time. And from what Meriel said, they didn't have any time left.

"Where is he?" asked Ellis again.

Meriel tried to remember. Sometimes, when she came back to her own body, she could remember exactly what it was like, being a fox, or rabbit. Sometimes she could remember nothing at all. Most often, she remembered bits.

She remembered the pain all right. It made her wince even now. Jet's mind had been filled with it.

"There was darkness," she murmured, "a circle of light."

She bit her lip. She'd seen that before, through another animal's eyes.

Then it clicked. "I know!" she cried. "I bet he's in an old rabbit burrow!"

"You're a genius!" said Ellis. They slapped palms. The rabbit burrows were over where the sand was firmer and held together with rough dune grass.

"Come on!" said Ellis. Meriel had narrowed down their search. But there were still lots of rabbit burrows to check. Hundreds maybe.

But then his sharp eyes saw another line of tracks. They were fresh too. But these made the hairs rise on the back of his neck.

"Cat tracks!" said Ellis. "Like those big ones I saw in the tunnels."

"The ginger tomcat," said Meriel.

"He's stalking something," said Ellis.

Somehow, the cat had sensed the gulls had gone. And he'd come out hunting.

"He's stalking Jet," said Meriel. Cats always knew where a bird lay wounded. Even if it crept into a rabbit burrow.

"Can't you stop him?" said Ellis frantically.

"You know I can't!" snapped Meriel.

She couldn't influence what an animal did. All she could do was share its life for a short while – feel what it felt, see what it saw.

"It's a special talent," Prof. Talltrees often told her. "Passed down through your family for generations. It's a precious gift, a privilege."

So why, to Meriel, did it sometimes seem more like a curse?

Ellis was already scrambling up the dune. She raced after him. Below them, going down into the dip, up the other side, was a perfect line of cat paw prints. You didn't need to be a tracker to follow them.

"He's going faster," said Ellis.

That meant the cat wasn't just following a scent. He'd heard Jet's cries – he knew exactly where the wounded gull was hiding.

"There he is!" said Ellis. They could see his ginger back, arching through the rippling grass. He was a very, very big cat.

Meriel looked around for a rock to throw. Couldn't see one. So she started to yell, clap her hands: "Shoo, cat! Get lost!"

The cat turned, gave them one scornful glance. He didn't care about them. He was as wild and bold as a tiger. His hunger made him bolder still. He knew he could snatch his prey and be off, before these humans even reached him.

He turned his back and padded on.

"*Shhh!*" hissed Ellis to Meriel. "Stay back."

He dropped to all fours, crawled through the grass, as stealthy as a cat, scarcely moving the grass. He parted the grass stems and peered out.

The cat was frozen, in that second before it pounces. Jet was huddled just inside the rabbit burrow.

As he saw this, in the same heart-stopping second, Ellis knew he was too late. Even if he dived, he couldn't reach the cat in time. One claw swipe, one bite from its jaws, could finish Jet off.

Ellis put the back of his hand to his mouth. Sucked on his skin. It made a shrill squeaking sound. The sound of a dying rabbit.

The cat's head whipped round. Rabbit! It looked back to Jet, then to where Ellis was hiding. It was confused now. It was spoiled for choice.

Those few moments of delay were enough for Meriel. She hadn't stayed back, of course, like Ellis had told her. She came hurtling out of the grass, shrugging off her jacket. In one swift movement, she yanked Jet out of the rabbit hole, scooped him up in her coat. Then staggered down the dune, carrying him in both arms.

He tried to peck her. She held on – he was too weak to even break her skin. Ellis came out of the grass. The tomcat snarled, showed its teeth, but backed off. Then it vanished like a ghost into the dunes.

"Is he alive?" said Ellis.

Meriel unwrapped her coat.

The Great Black-backed Gull seemed small and shrunken. He'd stopped even trying to peck now. His eyes were shut. His coral-pink feet were tucked in close to his body.

Ellis made a small hissing sound through his teeth. Meriel knew what that meant. It meant, "It doesn't look good."

"Let's go and find Danny." Meriel sighed. At least she'd done what she promised. She'd found Jet.

But they didn't have to find Danny. Danny found them. He came racing through the dunes with TJ and Cal.

Panting, he skidded to a stop. He saw the bundle in Meriel's arms. "Jet!" You could see he didn't dare ask, "Is he still alive?" So Meriel told him.

"He's alive," she said. "Just."

Danny reached out a hand to stroke Jet's drooping head. But then he drew it back, as if he thought Jet's hold on life was so fragile, that even one light touch might finish him off.

"Don't be scared," said Meriel. "He's not dead yet. He's tough."

So Danny dared to stroke Jet's head, crooning soothing words under his breath as if the wounded gull were a sick child.

Ellis stared, shook his head. *If we both live a hundred years*, he was thinking, *I'll never know Meriel.* Before, she'd been so cold and indifferent she seemed cruel. But now, in her own way, was she actually trying to comfort Danny?

But there was no time to waste wondering: "We'd better get Jet back to Professor Talltrees," Ellis told them, "as fast as we can."

And there was another reason they had to leave quickly. Suddenly, from beyond the dunes came savage howls. Ellis felt the hairs prickle on the back of his neck. "What on earth is that?"

"It's the slaves," said TJ.

After Cal had set them free, some slaves had stayed huddled in the church, too scared to come out. Some had wandered outside, dazed and shell-shocked. Some had returned to their homes. But others had gathered in an angry mob and armed themselves with rocks and sticks.

Over a distant dune, a ragged slave appeared.

"Get down!" said Ellis. They crouched in the dune grass. Meriel hugged Jet closer to protect him.

The slave stared around, waved his stick wildly.

"What's he doing?" hissed Ellis.

"Probably hunting for gulls," said Meriel in her matter-of-fact voice. "Or for Creepers."

"But I set the slaves free," protested Cal. "I was on their side. They won't hurt me."

"I wouldn't bet on it," said Meriel. She'd heard those kind of cries before, from animals goaded beyond endurance. "They're half crazy. They're out of control."

More arms waving weapons appeared above the dune.

"Come on!" said Ellis, urgently. But Cal insisted, "I'll just explain to them. Explain that I hated being a Creeper."

There was another blood-chilling shriek. "Are you joking?" Ellis yelled into Cal's face. "Do you think they'll listen? They'll rip you and Jet to pieces. Probably rip us all to pieces!"

Cal hesitated. Then hurried after the others into the dunes.

"Are they coming after us?" said Ellis. "Did they see us?" His mind was racing. This was a complication he hadn't thought of – the slaves out for revenge.

Frantically, he scanned the map of Mackenzie Point he had in his head. Somehow, they had to reach that crumbling path to the mainland. But how could they do that without being chased and attacked? "We've got a problem," he muttered to Meriel.

Meanwhile, Cal was plunging ahead through the dune grass. "This way!" he yelled, over his shoulder.

"That's the wrong direction!" called Ellis.

Cal's voice came back faintly.

"What's he say?" asked Ellis.

"Something about a boat," Meriel answered.

Fifteen minutes later, Cal was rowing them like a maniac back to the mainland. He'd found them a Creepers' boat. He was lucky to get it – it was the only one left. The others had been taken by Creepers fleeing Mackenzie Point.

Halfway between Mackenzie Point and the mainland, Cal stopped, shattered. As he slumped over the oars, the others could see that creepy red eye, staring at them from his shaved head. Cal had tried and tried to rub it away. But it still hadn't gone completely.

"I'll take over," said Danny, making the boat rock as he leaped off his seat. He was mad with impatience to get Jet back to Prof. Talltrees. If anyone could save Jet, he could.

"No, sit down," gasped Cal. "I'm all right. I'll get you there."

His arm muscles were cracking with strain. But he forced them to pull even harder.

They reached Sea Haven in record time and dragged the boat up the pebbly beach.

"There's a train to the city every hour," said Danny. "But I've got no money for the fare."

"We've got money," said Ellis. "Don't worry about that."

"Then let's go," begged Danny. "We've got to get Jet to the Prof."

As he spoke, he sneaked a look at Jet. Jet's eyes were closed, his head lolling. Meriel asked Danny, "Do you want to carry him?" But Danny shook his head. "No, you do it," he said. He couldn't bear to. What if Jet died in his arms?

They were hurrying towards the train station, when suddenly Cal said, "Wait!"

Ellis turned back. "What's the matter?"

"Me and TJ aren't coming," said Cal.

"What?" said Ellis, surprised. He'd just assumed they'd all be going back to the Natural History Museum.

TJ was as surprised as Ellis. "So where are we going?" he asked his big brother. Where *could* they go? The only home they'd ever known was Mackenzie Point.

Cal shuffled about in his big welly boots, rubbed for the hundredth time at that red eye. Then he dropped a bombshell. "Mum's living here, in Sea Haven."

TJ gaped at him in silence for what seemed like ages. Then he burst out, "You're kidding me!" Somehow he'd thought his mum was unreachable, on the other side of the world.

But Cal was nodding his big head so hard, it seemed he might shake it off. "It's true! I swear!"

TJ stared at his brother some more. Then he got angry. A torrent of questions poured from his mouth. "Has Mum been here all the time? Why didn't you tell me? How did you find out? How long have you known?"

Cal looked confused and upset. He only answered the last two questions. "Someone from Sea Haven told me she moved here – just before the gulls came."

"Have you been to see her?" demanded TJ.

The two brothers seemed to have forgotten the others existed. Ellis shot a puzzled glance at Meriel. She shrugged back. She was as much in the dark as he was. She only knew this was family business – something she didn't understand.

"Have you been to see Mum?" demanded TJ again. "Without me?"

Cal shook his head. "I just walked past her house," he told TJ. "I didn't dare knock. I thought, *What if Dad finds out I've been to see her? He'll go mental.* But Dad can't stop us now."

TJ's face was twisted between hope and fear.

"But what if Dad isn't dead?" he whispered. "We don't *know* he is, not for a fact."

Meriel raised an eyebrow at Ellis. That meant, "Shall we tell them?"

Ellis took a deep breath. "There was a chain up on the tower," he said. "I chucked it at Red Eye. This big gold thing with medallions..."

"Dad's chain," interrupted TJ. "It's got to be."

His Dad never went anywhere without it. He just couldn't accept that Mackenzie Point was doomed, even before the gulls came. That it was crumbling away. That soon he'd be Mayor of nothing but sand and waves and sea.

TJ stared again into Cal's face. And he knew they were both thinking the same thing. That Dad would never be parted from his chain, not while he had any breath left in his body. To the two brothers, it was certain proof that Dad was never coming back.

TJ looked sad and grave, like he knew he should.

But then he turned aside, secretly closed his eyes and breathed out a long, guilty sigh of relief.

"Come on," said Cal, putting a hand on TJ's shoulder. "I'll show you where Mum lives."

"Think she'll be pleased to see us?" worried TJ. "What if she's not in?"

They went walking off, their heads close together, talking. At the last minute, TJ remembered to turn around and wave and shout, "Catch up with you later!"

"Are we going now?" fumed Danny. He couldn't help it but, at this moment, he didn't care about TJ and Cal's problems. All he cared about was Jet.

Danny, Ellis and Meriel caught the five o'clock train back to the city. Meriel kept Jet on her knee, bundled up in her jacket. They bought drinks and sandwiches from the snack trolley. Ellis felt at the rake wound on his neck. *Ouch*, he thought. *That hurts*. Was his face as big a mess as Danny's? All covered in claw marks and scratches?

Meriel munched her sandwich. She scowled round the carriage. "Why is everyone staring at us?" she asked Ellis.

"Maybe because we look like we've been in a war," Ellis answered.

Chapter
Sixteen

An hour later, Danny, Ellis and Meriel were down in
the cellars and corridors under the Natural History
Museum, where Prof. Talltrees studied the bones of
extinct animals. But now he had a living creature on
his laboratory bench.

Danny watched as the Prof cleaned Jet's wounds,
dabbed on antiseptic. Danny didn't say anything. He
was in awe of the tall gangling professor, with his

eyepatch and badly scarred face. He had an air of authority, even though his voice was quiet, his hands gentle.

But then the Prof spread out Jet's useless wing and said, "It's a bad break. I might not be able to fix it."

"But you'll try, won't you?" Danny burst out.

The Prof considered saying something like, "He could die anyway, from his other injuries." Or, "If a gull can't fly, it's kinder to put him down."

But one look at Danny's distressed face made him change his mind.

"I'll try," he said. "At least you got him here quickly – before infection set in."

With skilful fingers, Prof. Talltrees cut out two cardboard splints for Jet's broken wing. Danny watched every movement.

"Hold this, please," said the Prof to Danny, handing him a roll of tape. "Cut me off some strips."

The Prof wrapped Sellotape around the cardboard splints, then fitted them to either side of Jet's wing. Then he taped the wing to Jet's body so he couldn't move it. Through all this, Jet didn't struggle. His eyes were shut. His head hung limply.

"Is he dead?" Danny kept asking.

"No," the Prof reassured him. "I can feel his heart beating."

Finally, the Prof put Jet, wrapped in a towel, in a cardboard box, with high sides, so he couldn't get out.

"That's all I can do," he said. "Now we just have to wait."

"I'll wait here with him," said Danny.

The Prof was going to say, "It won't make any difference." Danny looked done-in. He needed a sleep, cleaning up, something to eat. But he could see that Danny was determined. That he'd probably stay here all night.

"All right," said the Prof. "I've got a camp bed. I'll bring that down. And some food."

Later, while Danny watched over Jet, Ellis, Meriel and the Prof were in the kitchen.

"I need a shower," said Ellis. That fishy gull stink was on his clothes, in his hair. It was turning his stomach. He wandered off to the bathroom.

"Hey, me first!" Meriel shouted after him. She leaped up. She was going to dash past Ellis, beat him to the shower, when the Prof said, "Wait a minute, Meriel. I want to talk, just me and you."

168

The Prof sat down at the kitchen table, taking the weight off his bad leg. He waved Meriel into the chair opposite, pushed a can of drink across the table towards her. She ripped off the ring pull and gulped it down.

"I've got the basics," said the Prof, "about what happened at Mackenzie Point." Danny had told him, when he took him some food. "Danny says you're both heroes."

Meriel gave a scornful snort. *"Huh!* We messed up this mission. At least, I did."

"Not what I heard," said the Prof.

"You heard wrong!" Meriel leaped out of her chair, paced about like a caged tiger.

"Well, let's hear your version," said the Prof.

Meriel stomped on the empty drink can, sent it skittering towards the waste bin. Her eyes blazed at the Prof with a fierce, unblinking stare. The kind of stare wolves use to try to intimidate you.

But the Prof knew her tricks. He stared back, calmly.

With a shrug, Meriel lowered her eyes, sat down.

"Start with Red Eye," said the Prof. "Tell me what you thought of him."

Meriel fidgeted some more. Finally she spoke. "I felt sorry for him," she said.

It was a good job Danny wasn't listening. He'd have freaked out, shouted, "Am I hearing right? You felt *sorry* for that evil psycho gull? You're kidding me!"

Red Eye had a list of crimes as long as your arm. He'd terrorized Mackenzie Point. He'd hurt, even killed people. If he didn't do it himself, he'd made it happen.

Even the Prof was surprised: "But didn't Red Eye try to kill you?"

Meriel frowned some more. "I still felt sorry for him," she said defiantly. "Because there was nobody like him in the world. Because he *knew* he was a freak!"

The Prof nodded slowly. Now he understood perfectly why Meriel felt sympathy for Red Eye. Because she often felt like a freak herself.

Ellis came back from the shower in fresh clothes, scrubbing with a towel at his wet hair. He stopped abruptly at the kitchen door. Trackers are really good at sensing atmosphere. He thought, *They've been talking about something serious.*

But, as soon as she saw him, Meriel bounced up. She wasn't the brooding kind. She lived like animals do, in the present. She shook off the memory of what it had been like, being Red Eye: his terrible loneliness, the black hole where his heart should have been. He'd had power but nothing else. Nothing else at all.

"About time!" she said to Ellis, shooting past him towards the shower.

"And don't use my shower gel!" he yelled after her.

Chapter
Seventeen

It was one month after the epic battle between Jet and Red Eye. After Red Eye had plunged into the sea, tangled up in a golden chain.

Mackenzie Point was like a ghost town. All its houses were abandoned. Sand blew into the windows and piled up inside. Soon, the buildings would slip into the sea, or be just ruins in the dunes.

Everyone had moved to the mainland. They'd always known they'd have to leave, sooner or later. Red Eye's reign of terror had just made it sooner. No one could bear to stay. The place had too many bad memories. And how could Creepers and slaves live happily side by side? As if nothing had happened?

Like all the rest, Cal and TJ had left Mackenzie Point. They were living at Sea Haven with their mum, all getting to know each other again. By now, Cal and TJ knew Dad was never coming back. They'd stopped jumping when they heard the front door open.

Danny was over there too, at Sea Haven. Mum's biker boyfriend had a house there. When he and Mum came back from their round-the-world trip, she'd moved in with him. And they'd decorated a bedroom for Danny, made it really nice.

Mum told Danny, "I'm tired of travelling. I'm staying in Sea Haven."

"Oh yeah?" Danny had said, dubiously. He'd heard that before. But he got on well with her biker boyfriend.

"I like him," Danny told Granddad. "He's a good guy. He's showing me how to strip down a bike."

Granddad was out of hospital. And he was the only person who still lived on Mackenzie Point. He wouldn't leave Wonderland. "Not until it falls into the sea," he'd told Danny.

"Stubborn old so-and-so," Danny's Mum had said.

But Danny understood. He spent a lot of time over there with Granddad. It was only a short boat ride from Sea Haven. On this trip, he'd brought a boatload of other people – Ellis, Meriel and Prof. Talltrees. These days, the Prof rarely left the city museum. But this was a very special occasion. They were going to set Jet free. Jet had finally recovered and his wing had healed. But would he be able to fly again?

"What are we waiting for?" asked Meriel. She wasn't just being her usual twisty self. She really couldn't stand the tension. What if Jet's wing wouldn't work? What if he couldn't swoop and soar and skim the wave tops? They'd have to feed him, keep him captive. He'd be dragging a crippled wing around for the rest of his life. What kind of life was that for a wild creature?

He'd be better off dead, Meriel decided.

"We're waiting for Cal and TJ," Ellis reminded her. They had to be there when Jet was released. "They won't be long."

Cal had got a job on a fishing boat. Already they'd made him first mate. He was a natural-born sailor. He'd be skipper of his own boat one day.

Meriel paced about. They were inside Wonderland, with all Danny's granddad's old arcade machines.

Granddad and the Prof were getting on really well. Granddad had shown him the laughing clown, the grabbing claw and the machine that told your fortune. Now the Prof was trying out Granddad's rifle range.

"Look at that!" said Danny.

The Prof, even with just one good eye, was a crack shot. He'd hit another bullseye.

"Wish those guns hadn't been locked away when Red Eye was here," said Danny.

"Come on!" Ellis said. "You mean, you'd have taken a shot at him? Remember what happened to the Mayor?"

Danny shrugged, as if to say, "I wouldn't have missed." He chewed nervously at his nails. Like

Meriel, he couldn't settle down. Jet was on the table, shut up in a cat's travelling basket. Danny couldn't even look at him. He knew he should be grateful Jet was still alive. It had been touch and go sometimes. Only the Prof's skill had pulled him through. But even the Prof didn't know if Jet would be able to fly.

"I can't promise anything," he'd told Danny. "We'll have to wait and see." But he'd prepared Danny for the worst. "Wings are complicated structures. Even now it's healed, it might be no good for flying. It all depends on how the bones have set."

"Where are Cal and TJ?" Danny fretted. "They should be here by now!" And he went rushing out of Wonderland, down to the shore to look out for their boat.

The Prof walked over from the rifle range to join Ellis and Meriel.

"It seems I've won this," he told them, grinning. He was hugging a giant-sized furry toy – an orange gorilla with long clingy arms. He was delighted with it, like a little kid.

The Prof's a strange guy, thought Ellis.

He seemed like a reserved and solemn boffin who only cared about bones. But, when you got to know him, he wasn't like that at all. He was full of surprises.

Danny came bursting back in. "They're here! They're here!"

Everyone hurried outside, the Prof carrying Jet in his basket. As if he could smell the sea, Jet was giving little cries: "*Kiaow, kiaow.*"

They took Jet past the roller coaster and Big Wheel. No gulls roosted there now. There had been a few, who'd stayed behind to raise their chicks. Now even they had gone, as if the place had bad memories for them too.

The Prof led his little group past the wire fence of Wonderland, into the dunes.

He pulled on a pair of old leather gloves. Jet was no longer a sad, wounded bundle of feathers. He was fighting fit, desperate to be free. The Prof lifted the basket lid, just a little. A yellow hatchet beak poked out through the gap and tried to peck him.

"*Whoa*, calm down, boy," said the Prof.

Cal came striding up from the beach where he'd left his boat, with TJ racing in front.

They didn't know the Prof. But Danny was too impatient to make any polite introductions. He just said, "Right! We're all here. Can we let him go now?"

The Prof was about to get Jet out of the basket. Suddenly he changed his mind.

"Do you want to do it?" he asked Danny, handing him the gloves.

"I won't need those," said Danny. But he put them on anyway.

With the big clumsy gloves on, he lifted Jet out of the basket. Jet squirmed in his grip, stabbed at the gloves. He was a big gull, awkward to handle.

"Hey, Jet, it's me," said Danny, trying to soothe him.

Danny lifted his hands high in the air. His arms were trembling. He felt his heart hammering wildly. Jet began trying out his wings, with a few creaky, stiff flaps. Danny let go, his eyes already gazing skywards.

But Jet tumbled into the soft sand.

Danny stared down, astonished. Despite all the warnings, he'd still believed the Prof could work miracles.

He watched Jet flopping about, trying to fly. It was heartbreaking. He just lost it. "You promised!" he roared at the Prof. "You promised!"

"No, he didn't," said Meriel, rushing to the Prof's defence.

Ellis backed her up. "He definitely didn't."

Danny turned on them savagely. But then, for some reason, he transferred his anger to Jet.

"Fly!" he bawled at Jet. "You useless, lazy bird!"

No one said anything. Cal took off his baseball cap. The red eye had faded now. But he rubbed at the spot on his bristly head where it had been.

"Fly!" raged Danny at Jet, almost in tears.

"Shut up a minute," said Ellis. "Give him time."

Jet was flexing his mended wing. He hopped and fluttered. He flapped it more strongly. Then, suddenly, he took off.

"Yes!" yelled Danny.

Jet was soaring now over Mackenzie Point, swooping, diving, just for the joy of it.

"Go, Jet!" screamed TJ, mad with excitement.

The Prof gave a long, secret sigh of relief. He glanced at Ellis and Meriel. "Lucky," mouthed Ellis.

They both knew, as well as the Prof, that Jet's chances of flying again hadn't been great.

But now Danny wanted something else.

He wanted Jet to come back to him, not fly off somewhere where he'd never see him again.

He told himself off for it. *Aren't you ever satisfied? Wasn't it enough that Jet was flying again?*

But it must have been Danny's lucky day; the day when all his wishes came true. For Jet, who was just a dot in the sky, came drifting gracefully back down on the thermals. He hovered overhead, then landed on top of a dune, watching Danny with bright, curious eyes.

"Hey, welcome back, Jet," said Danny, trying to sound cool and casual, while his heart was bursting with happiness.

An hour later, Ellis went looking for Meriel. She'd wandered off from Wonderland, where Danny's granddad had made lunch, frying sausages for everyone.

He tracked her easily, by her footprints. He knew them as well as he knew his own. He found her standing alone by the shore. She had her back to him. She was staring out to sea.

"Didn't you want anything to eat?" he asked her.

He wasn't surprised she'd done a runner. She couldn't handle being with too many people.

"We're going back now," he said. "You ready?"

Meriel still didn't reply, or turn round. She didn't seem aware that Ellis existed.

Ellis thought, *She's in a trance*. He wasn't surprised about that either. Meriel often escaped from people by going into an animal's mind.

Maybe she'd seen a dolphin, far out to sea. Meriel had a lot of time for dolphins. She said they were more civilized than humans.

But when he saw her face, he knew she wasn't in a trance. Her eyes didn't have that glazed, faraway look. Then they fixed on something at her feet, among the shells and seaweed. It glittered like gold. At first, Ellis couldn't see what it was. He kicked some seaweed aside.

He felt his heart clench. "It's the Mayor's chain. How did that get here?"

Meriel stared at him. And he was shocked to see that her eyes held a kind of sick terror.

"You don't think he's still alive, do you?" she asked him.

"What? Red Eye? Come on!" Ellis laughed, uneasily. "Danny saw him drown in the sea."

But Meriel, who'd experienced the full power of Red Eye's mind, thought he was capable of anything.

"What do you think he is, Houdini?" said Ellis. "That he could escape from that chain underwater?" He laughed again. At the same time, he felt his spine touched by icy fingers.

But Meriel seemed to be reassured. "Yeah, you're right. It must have got unwrapped from his dead body somehow, washed ashore."

"Fish will have eaten him by now," said Ellis. "There'll be nothing left."

But even as he said this, he found himself swinging round, staring back at the town, to that high tower. As if he expected to see Red Eye perching there, on his favourite west-facing dragon. To hear his harsh war cry, *"Kwarr! Kwarr!"* echoing again over Mackenzie Point.

"This is stupid!" said Ellis, angrily. "He's dead. Right? I mean, you can't mind-read him, can you? You can't pick up any trace?" He looked intently into Meriel's face.

She shook her head. "No." She didn't add, "But

I never could." After all, Red Eye was the one who'd invaded *her* mind. He'd never let her into his.

At least Ellis was reassured. "Well, that's it, then," he said. "He's definitely fish food."

As he said that, on the wind from Wonderland, came peal after peal of mocking laughter. Meriel gazed at Ellis, startled. "What's that?" The sick terror was in her eyes again.

"It's only Danny's granddad," said Ellis. "Showing the Prof that creepy clown."

He frowned and looked down at the chain. "What do we do with that? Shall we take it back for TJ and Cal? It belonged to their dad."

"No!" said Meriel, suddenly back to her usual fierce self. "Chuck it back in the sea!"

Before Danny could object, she'd grabbed the chain and hurled it. It writhed in the air like a golden snake. Then fell sparkling into the waves.

She rubbed her hands together, as if she was rubbing away Red Eye.

"I'm ready now," said Meriel, striding off towards the boats. "Let's go home."

* * *

Somewhere out over the Atlantic, a storm was raging. A great white bird flew on through the rain and wind. It reached the coast. It hung in the sky like an avenging angel, looking down. There were lots of tiny, remote fishing towns down there, tucked away, on islands, headlands, inlets.

It made its choice.

As it hurtled down a savage cry echoed through the heavens.

"KWARR!"

DON'T MISS

ANIMAL INVESTIGATORS

MISSION 2:

GHOST DOGS

Read on for a sneak preview...

Chapter One

The boy came skidding into the kitchen of the children's care home. The cook looked up from the soup he was stirring.

"Hey," the cook greeted the boy. "What's your hurry? She after you again?"

She was the matron of the children's care home. She hated the boy. She saw it as her personal duty to civilize him.

Leon the cook was his only protector. Every time the boy was in trouble with the matron, he ran to Leon in the kitchen. Or sometimes, he ran out to the kennel outside and curled up with Tyson, the care home dog.

The boy was about four years old. No one knew his age exactly because he'd been dumped, two years ago, outside the care home. He'd had a piece of paper pinned to his coat. It said, *Look after him. His name is Blue.*

That had annoyed the matron right away. "Why is he called Blue?" she'd said. "What kind of stupid name is that for a boy?"

Blue sat down at the kitchen table.

"Want a drink?" asked Leon.

Blue nodded. He could speak, as well as any other four year old. But he didn't often choose to.

Leon poured Blue some milk into a plastic mug. The old man liked Blue. But even he had to admit that the boy was strange. Even stranger than the matron realized. She hated Blue because of his defiance – the way he stared at her with those icy blue eyes, as if she was something nasty he'd trodden in. But, if she'd known about what else he did, she'd have a fit.

"Don't try any of your tricks now," Leon warned Blue. "*She* might come in. Remember, they're a secret between you and me."

Blue stared back at him. His eyes made even Leon shiver. They chilled you right through to the bone. Apart from that, he looked like a nice, normal little boy. His nails were kept clean, his hair short, his face well-scrubbed, like all the other care home kids.

But he wasn't normal. Normal kids couldn't do what Blue was doing now.

"Hey, I told you not to do that stuff," said Leon. But it was no good. Blue never took any notice. He just stared at you and did what he liked. That's what made Matron so mad, made her want to break his spirit.

Blue had turned his gaze to his milk. He stuck a spoon in it. Then fixed the mug with those frosty eyes. And the milk froze. It turned solid. Blue knocked it out of the mug onto the table. And using the spoon as a stick, he licked it, like a lollipop.

"How d'you do it?" said Cook. "Make the temperature drop like that?" Frost shimmered on the table too, as if Blue had made his own mini-winter.

Blue shrugged. He had no idea where his strange powers came from.

"Heck of a party trick," said the cook, shaking his head and grinning.

The kitchen door flew open. "What's going on here?" Matron's suspicious gaze swept round the kitchen. She saw Blue eating his lollipop. "Why aren't you at school?" she demanded.

Blue shot her a scornful look, then wriggled out of the open kitchen window.

"That boy!" said the matron. "He'll be the death of me."

She caught up with Blue out in the yard. He'd gone to his second refuge, the dog kennel. He was curled up inside, with Tyson, the old Alsatian.

"Come out of there!" ordered Matron, kneeling down. She reached into the kennel and hauled Tyson out by his collar. It was a worn blue collar, with a metal tag on it, engraved with his name and the care home address.

"You old bag of bones," she said to Tyson. "It's about time we had you put down. You're half dead anyway."

Then Matron made an even bigger mistake. In her bad temper, she slapped the old dog on the nose. Tyson yelped, piteously.

Blue came crawling out of the kennel. He stood up.

"Now I've got you," said the matron. "And don't stare at me like that! Like you'd like to kill me!"

But Blue never took his eyes off her. Suddenly, Matron felt the air around her getting chilly. Which was strange because it was a blazing hot summer's day. She felt something cold on her lips, in her hair. White flakes whirled around her. Surely it couldn't be? Not snowflakes? Then she was shivering, her teeth chattering. Her breath turned to crackling ice crystals. She watched in horror, as her own hands turned blue.

A last crazy thought flashed through her head. *So that's why they named him Blue.*

Then her eyes glazed over and she slumped to the ground.

Blue took one quick look at the matron's body, dusted with snow. Then he said, "Come on Tyson. Let's go."

The boy and the dog took off down the road. They crossed a bridge over a river. Then passed a sign that said, *Welcome to Forest Edge. Please Drive Carefully.*

But Blue didn't want to go to the town. He wanted to get as far away from people as possible. But first, he took off his shirt and sweater, his socks and shoes and put them in a neat pile on the river bank.

Then he and Tyson turned right, went down a dirt track and plunged into the forest. Soon, the trees swallowed them up.

To find out what happens next read

GHOST DOGS

Coming soon...

For more thrilling
mystery adventures
log on to
www.fiction.usborne.com